ARCADE

AND THE FIERY METAL TESTER

Also by Rashad Jennings

The IF in Life

THE COIN SLOT CHRONICLES SERIES

Book 1: *Arcade and the Triple T Token*
Book 2: *Arcade and the Golden Travel Guide*

ARCADE

AND THE FIERY METAL TESTER

RASHAD JENNINGS

WITH JILL OSBORNE

ZONDERKIDZ

Arcade and the Fiery Metal Tester
Copyright © 2020 by Rashad Jennings, LLC
Illustrations © 2020 Rashad Jennings

Requests for information should be addressed to:
Zonderkidz, *3900 Sparks Dr. SE, Grand Rapids, Michigan 49546*

Library of Congress Cataloging-in-Publication Data

Names: Jennings, Rashad, 1985- author. | Osborne, Jill, 1961- author.
Title: Arcade and the fiery metal tester / Rashad Jennings, with Jill Osborne.
Description: Grand Rapids, Michigan: Zonderkidz, 2020. | Series: The coin slot chronicles;
    3 | Audience: Ages 8–12. | Summary: As New York City experiences the hottest
    summer on record, eleven-year-old Arcade Livingston is tested like never before to use
    the Triple T token's powerful ways to outsmart a bully, find a place for his best friend to
    live, and spy on some pesky villains from the 1900s.
Identifiers: LCCN 2019038439 (print) | LCCN 2019038440 (ebook) | ISBN
9780310767459 (hardback) | ISBN 9780310767466 (epub)
Subjects: CYAC: Adventure and adventurers—Fiction. | Friendship—Fiction. | Brothers
    and sisters—Fiction. | Magic—Fiction. | New York (N.Y.)—Fiction. | African
    Americans—Fiction.
Classification: LCC PZ7.1.J4554 An 2020 (print) | LCC PZ7.1.J4554 (ebook) | DDC
    [Fic]—dc23
LC record available at https://lccn.loc.gov/2019038439
LC ebook record available at https://lccn.loc.gov/2019038440

Illustrated by: Alan Brown
Art direction: Cindy Davis
Interior design: Denise Froehlich

Printed in the United States of America

19 20 21 22 23 LSC 10 9 8 7 6 5 4 3 2 1

*To the joy of our hearts and the future
of our world—THE KIDS . . .*

*As I did with books one and two, I also dedicate to
you this third book of The Coin Slot Chronicles—
Arcade and The Fiery Metal Tester. I trust
you've already read The Triple T Token and The
Golden Travel Guide. If not, I highly recommend
you do. They truly help you begin to understand
the mysterious people, places, and things Arcade
experiences. And in this book, things really begin to
heat up! So you might want to read it in a cool place!*

*I'd like to also dedicate this book to you, the amazing
parents, teachers, librarians, and school administrators.
You are truly instrumental in making my school
visits and book signings an absolute pleasure!*

*Finally, for all who will read my words, I pray that
something in the pages of this third book of Arcade's
incredible adventures will find its way to the center
of your heart, and that it sets ablaze within you
the desire to let nothing keep you from your great
quest of becoming the best version of yourself . . .*

Again, happy travels!

CHAPTER 1

102nd Floor

"Arcade, QUIT pushing the elevator buttons! You *don't* have control over them."

"CHILL, Zoe! I think by now I know what I'm doing."

"No, you DON'T. This is the *Empire State Building*, not one of your arcade token adventures."

I stepped back from the button panel and wrapped my hand around the Triple T Token that was hanging from the gold chain around my neck. It had been in my possession almost six months now—heating up and pulsing whenever it felt like it, taking my friends and me on journeys around the world, into my past, and even into my future! Today, the token kept its cool, hanging there like any medallion would. *That* was a relief. I stared at the display above the elevator doors.

78, 79, 80 . . .

My older sister, Zoe, and I were on our way up to the top of the Empire State Building to meet our parents. They had left a note for us on the dining room table that hot, August morning:

Zoe and Arcade,
Meet us at 1:00 pm on top of the Empire
State Building. Tickets are in the attached
envelope. We will have our annual back-to-
school goals talk there!
                    Love, Mom and Dad

And now it was 12:45. Dad always says that on time is
late, so our only option was to be early. Especially since we
were going to have the dreaded *goals talk*.

"This is a pretty smooth elevator ride." Zoe bit her pinkie
nail while she drummed her fingers on her bent elbow.

"You nervous?"

"Me?" Zoe pointed her thumb at her chest. "Why
should I be nervous?"

"Goals . . . back to school . . . talks with parents . . ."

Ding!

The elevator doors opened. We stepped out and were
greeted by a smiling lady whose badge said her name was
Marjorie.

"Welcome to the 86th floor."

I grinned. "Thanks! But doesn't this building have 102
floors? I'm pretty sure I read that in a fifty-pound coffee
table book I checked out from the library."

Her eyes brightened. "*New York City: A Coffee Table
Tour?*"

"Yeah, that's the one!" I pointed my index finger toward
the sky.

Zoe rolled her eyes.

Marjorie continued. "I have that book at home. It's a favorite. And you're *quite right*, young man. There are 102 floors. What's your name?"

"Arcade Livingston." I held my hand out to shake hers. "Nice to meet you, ma'am."

"Arcade? What a magical name! Follow me, you two. The building narrows here, so you have to change to an elevator in the center to make it all the way to the top."

"So it's just like the subway, huh? I love it! Lead the way."

"Yeah, *just* like it." Zoe laughed. "Except we're *above* ground. *And* there are fewer people. *And* we're traveling vertically, not horizontally. Other than that, and a handful of other differences, it's *just* like the subway." Zoe cut in front of me, jostling me into the wall of the narrow hallway.

"What I *meant was*, it's like the subway because we have to *change cars*. When are you gonna start thinkin' like me so we don't keep having all these arguments?"

Zoe stopped and turned, crossing her arms. "Umm, never?!? And I prefer to call them *debates*."

"Of course you do."

Marjorie led us to a special elevator in the middle of the building. "Here you go, young people. Enjoy the rest of your ride. It's a beautiful day. You'll be able to see forever. And make sure you come back and check out the 86th floor open-air observation deck."

"We'll do that on the way down. Thank you, ma'am." I stepped into the elevator car and Zoe followed. The doors closed.

Ding!

I reached for Triple T. It was cool to the touch, just like it had been ever since the middle of June when Zoe and I returned from our cousins Celeste and Derek's house in Forest, Virginia. Cool was perfect. It had been the hottest summer ever recorded in New York City, and I needed some time to figure things out.

The display above the doors clicked away. *100, 101, 102 . . .*

I opened my mouth and tried to yawn. "Are your ears plugged?"

"Huh?" Zoe pressed her finger in front of her ear and wiggled it.

Ding!

"WHOA! That was the quickest elevator ride of my life!" I stepped forward. The doors opened, and this time we were greeted by a smiling gentleman named Reynold.

"Welcome to the top of the Empire State Building!

You're in luck. You're the only ones up here. That hardly ever happens."

"Really?" I stepped out of the elevator to have a look around. "This is dope!"

Zoe chewed away on her nail. "Are you sure there's not a married couple up here? Our parents are supposed to meet us at one o'clock."

Reynold shook his head. "Haven't seen 'em yet. And I see *everyone* who makes it up here to the top."

"Hmmm. I wonder if we should wait here for them." Zoe looked around and took her pink and purple tie-dyed backpack off her shoulders.

Reynold led us toward the enclosed, circular observatory. "Not necessary. Go ahead and enjoy the view. When they arrive, I'll let them know you're here."

"First one who finds the Times Square ball wins!" I yelled, and we both charged in opposite directions.

Zoe headed to the left side of the building, and I went right. No surprise there. I scanned the horizon filled with skyscrapers, water, ferries, and bridges below. I found the Statue of Liberty. It looked like the size of a chess piece!

"Whoa."

"There's the Brooklyn Bridge!" Zoe pointed out. I'd been over it in a taxi only once, but there was no mistaking it.

I wanted to keep staring out, but I had a game to win, and from all my study of the geography of Manhattan, I knew I was looking south. Times Square was north from here. I turned and made my way toward the other side of the building so I could beat my sister to the ball.

I raced alongside the windows, focused on the New York City skyline, but before I reached the north end of the observatory, I ran right into a little old woman wearing white sweats and a . . . Triple T ball cap! My mouth hung open. I had seen her only a few times before. And the first time I would never forget. It was at the Ivy Park library right after our move to New York City. That day she gave me the Triple T Token and told me, "Happy travels."

She sat there, knocked to the ground, her ball cap glowing with gold and silver glitter. "Arcade, you're getting big."

I reached out a hand to help her up. "I'm so sorry! I didn't see you there."

She stood, brushed herself off, and stared at me.

I looked around. Reynold was nowhere in sight. "How'd you get up here?"

"Elevator," she said, raising an eyebrow. "Just like the subway."

I laughed. "I like how you think."

"I like how *you* think. That's why you have the token."

"Yeeeeaaaahhhhh. About that. I have a LOT of questions for you, like—"

She put her hand on my chest. "Sorry, no time. But I do have to tell you one thing. Things are about to heat up. In all areas. To test your mettle."

My metal?

"It's all part of the process."

Process?

"Trust the tester . . ."

Tester?

"Arcade!" Zoe's voice echoed in the distance. "I found the ball! I win!" I turned to see Zoe standing by a window in the corner of the observation room. She had her phone out, taking pictures, no doubt to record the moment and have proof that she won.

"No! I hate losing to my sister!"

When I turned back toward the old woman, she was gone.

CHAPTER 2

#GOALZ

rcade! I beat you! I know it looks tiny, but that's it. The Times Square ball. I win!"

I stood there, gazing out the window, down, down, down at a little glowing ball.

"Arcade?"

Yep, that's the ball alright.

"Arcade?"

What did she mean, things were going to heat up?

"ARCADE!"

"That is seriously a *long way down*. Good thing Doug isn't here."

Zoe put a hand on her hip. "Aren't you going to acknowledge that I beat you?"

"Were we in a race? The thin air up here must be messing with your mind."

Zoe sighed and threw her head back. "You're impossible." She took a step back from the window and shielded her eyes from the sun. "It really *is* a good thing Doug isn't here."

Doug Baker is my best friend in New York City. He lives three doors down from our brownstone in Upper West Side Manhattan. Doug lives in a brownstone, too, but it's painted green. And he's deathly afraid of heights.

I scanned the northern view of Manhattan. "Wow. Central Park is huge! I can almost see the whole thing." I squinted and tried to zero in on the area where my new middle school, MS 230, was located, somewhere around W 93rd Street.

"Check it out, there's the Thanksgiving parade route!" Zoe pointed straight down. I followed her finger to a narrow street that bent sharply next to Macy's Department Store.

"They carry the big balloons down that street? Amazing." As I leaned into the window for a closer look, a hand rested on my shoulder.

"Have you ever seen a more spectacular view?" It was Dad, and he had his arm linked with Mom's.

If only I could tell you about the time on top of that Egyptian pyramid . . .

Mom moved in between Zoe and me and peered out the window. "I'm so proud that you made it here all by yourselves. You're so grown up! We thought this would be a great place to discuss your goals for the year."

Gulp.

Dad squeezed in between Mom and me. "But we're going simple this time. It's been a stressful year for all of us, and since we know you'll both do fine in your studies, we're focusing on two other things: building character and having fun." Dad glanced at me and raised an eyebrow.

Zoe stepped back from the window, ran both hands through her hair, and frowned. "Wait. No goals about grade point averages? Or trying different kinds of vegetables? Or learning a new skill?" She loves setting *those* kinds of goals.

"You heard your dad," Mom said, waving a hand in the air. "Character and fun."

I heaved a sigh of relief.

Dad stepped back next to Zoe and pulled up a memo app on his phone. "So, let's talk character. Zoe, what's a character trait that you would like to strengthen this year?"

"Zoe would like to become less bossy," I blurted out.

Zoey glared. "And Arcade would like to become more open to correction."

Mom shook her head. "That's not how it works. You may not set goals for each other."

"Yes, but it's *easier* that way." I gave Zoe a side glance and a smirk. She reached over and covered my face with her hand.

"Patience," Zoe said. "I need to be more patient. With Arcade, of course, but I also struggle waiting for things to fall into place."

Dad nodded. "And nothing has fallen into place in New York City?"

Zoe bit her lip. "Nothing yet."

Dad typed out some words on his phone. "Patience for Zoe. Got it." He looked back up, catching her glance. "And what would you like to do for fun?"

Zoe looked out toward Central Park and smiled. "I'd like to do some bird-watching in the Ramble."

"Ramble?" I stared out at the city. "What's that?"

"The Ramble. You know. It's that section of the park with all the twisty paths. We've been through there a couple times. I read that it's one of the top bird-watching locations in the United States."

"Sounds boring," I said.

Zoe pushed me in the shoulder. "It's NOT boring. In fact, there is quite a bit of adventure to be discovered in the Ramble. I heard there's a secret cave that's been closed to the public since the 1920s."

Hmmm. Secret cave?

Dad typed some more, then put his hand on Zoe's shoulder. "Great choice, Zoe. I think those two goals will go together nicely."

Mom stepped up next to me. "So how about you, Arcade? What character trait would you like to work on?"

I leaned my elbows against the window ledge, resting my chin in my hand. "Mom, this sounds a lot like a 'feelings' talk. Can't we just go with a GPA goal?"

"And what's wrong with feelings?" Zoe put a hand on her hip.

I shivered. "They're confusing. I like facts."

"Yeah? Like how many sides are on a stop sign?"

"That's easy. There's ten."

"No. There's eight."

"Ten."

"Really? Arcade, maybe you should focus on feelings more. Your facts are a little wonky."

"That's enough, you two." Dad looked up from

his phone and gave me a funny grin. "Hey, how about compassion?"

My token heated up a little. "Compassion?"

"Yes. We already know you're a kid who likes to help people. So somewhere in that eleven-year-old heart of yours are the seeds of great compassion. Maybe you'd like to grow in that area this year?"

Zoe pulled up the definition of compassion on her phone. "Compassion. A feeling—"

"Oh, here we go with the feelings! I told you—"

Zoe put her phone under my nose. "Ahem . . . a feeling of deep sympathy and sorrow for another who is stricken by misfortune, accompanied by a strong desire to alleviate the suffering." She looked up at me. "I agree with Dad. Compassion would be a good character goal for you."

I waited for her to end with a joke. A tease. An insult. *Anything.*

But there was only silence. With everyone just staring at me.

"Okay! But I don't *know* anyone who is . . . what did it say exactly? Stricken by misfortune?"

Dad approached the window and looked out over Manhattan. "Hmmm. I suppose that there might be *someone* out there in this city who's been stricken by a little misfortune, don't you think? And knowing you, son, you'll run right into them."

"Yep, knowing you . . ." Zoe snickered.

I elbowed her. "Fine. I'll take compassion."

Dad typed "compassion" into his phone.

"And how about the fun goal?" Mom breathed in deep as she took in the view. "Hey, check it out. There's Rockefeller Center. That's where they decorate the huge Christmas tree every year." She draped her arm over Dad's shoulder. "We should go to the tree lighting this year."

That gave me a fun goal idea.

"I'd like to experience New York City."

Zoe looked around. "Uh, duh. We've been living here for six months, Arcade."

"Yeah, but we haven't done any of the *fun stuff*. You know, the Statue of Liberty, Times Square . . . and this is the first time I've been to the top of the Empire State Building. I haven't even seen a Broadway show yet, and Dad *works* on Broadway!"

Dad dropped his chin. "I'm sorry, Arcade. Your mom and I have been so busy working. I guess we haven't been the greatest travel guides."

The Triple T Token sent a little shock through my body. *Not now!*

Dad typed in my fun goal: See New York City. "Okay, that's it. We're done."

"That's it? No wise speeches? Or famous quotes? How about a story from your youth?" Those things had been a big part of all our goal-setting meetings in the past. I scratched my head. "No prayer?"

Dad cracked a smile. "Oh, yeah, we're definitely going to have a prayer."

"Oh, good."

"And you can do it."

"ME?"

"YEAH."

"HERE?"

"I think it would be great for you to pray for the family." Mom moved in closer and grabbed my hand and Zoe's hand. Dad pulled in between Zoe and me. And there we were, getting ready to pray on the top of the Empire State Building!

They all bowed their heads. I looked around, expecting to see the Triple T woman staring at me. But we were the only ones up there. I bowed my head and cleared my throat. "Um, Lord . . . thank you for my family and for all the new experiences here in New York City. This year, please give us a new way of looking at things. Make Zoe more patient and show me how to have more compassion. And help us have fun while we do it. Amen."

CHAPTER 3

Falling into Place

So, are you two okay getting home? Dad and I have health checkups in an hour." Mom linked arms with Dad again as we waited for the first set of elevators to take us down to the 86th floor observation deck.

Reynold waved. "You got lucky, being up here all by yourselves. Come see us again soon!"

"Are you sure there wasn't anyone else up here this whole time?" I asked.

Like an old lady wearing white sweats and a Triple T ball cap?

Reynold stuck out a lip and shook his head. "Not on top of this building, son. Like I said, everyone who comes up here passes by me."

"Okay." I glanced around, looking for glitter. "Seems kinda weird."

Reynold held the doors open as my family entered. "It hardly ever happens, but when it does, I like to call it the Manhattan Miracle. It's like someone reserved the top of the Empire State Building just for your family today, for some special purpose. I'd start paying real close attention to what happens next."

"Thank you, Reynold," Mom said. "Have a blessed day."

The doors closed in front of us. As we descended to the 86th floor, our ears popping, I couldn't help but wonder what happened to that Triple T lady. And what in the world she meant by "test my metal."

The view from the 86th floor was awesome too. We couldn't see as much of Central Park, but there was a nice breeze outside to cool us down just a bit on such a hot day.

Mom checked her watch. "Oh, dear, we better be on our way. Do you kids want to stay a little longer?"

I wiped a little sweat drop from my forehead. "Nah. I'm ready to go."

"Me too." Zoe turned and headed toward the elevators. "And don't worry, Arcade and I will be fine getting home."

"Yeah, we're pretty much experts on the subway. And now, with my new 'fun' goal, I guess I need to pay attention to what's above ground too."

"Fair enough," Dad said. "Do you have rides left on your metro cards?"

Zoe and I both nodded.

Dad shook an index finger at us. "But even though you feel comfortable, you need to stay alert. Trouble can be anywhere. Keep an eye on one another and text me when you get home."

"*I'll* text you," Zoe said. "Arcade never knows where his phone is."

"Yes, I do!"

"Oh, yeah? Then where is it right now?"

I reached for the back pocket of my jeans.

Empty!

"Hey! I *know* I put it in there!"

"Ha!" Zoe held up my phone. "I pickpocketed you five minutes ago!"

"Give it back, zoo breath!"

Zoe laughed and handed it over. I slipped it in my back pocket.

Ding!

The elevator had arrived to take us down to the bottom floor. We all stepped in and had to crunch in with a crowd.

"Hey, Mom, what's the craziest elevator you've ever ridden?"

Mom looked up toward the elevator ceiling. "Hmmmm." Then she glanced over and gave Dad a funny look. "Must've been that time we rode one to Australia."

Dad's eyes widened.

"You rode one *to* Australia?" Triple T jumped inside my shirt.

Mom crunched her eyebrows together. "Oh, did I say *to*? I meant *in*. The craziest elevator ride was *in* Australia." Then she turned and looked straight ahead. But the look on her face told me there was more to the story. Much more.

"Zoe, I think Mom knows I have the Triple T Token."

Zoe and I bobbed and weaved through the crowd on the way to the 50th Street subway station.

"That's ridiculous. How could she know?" We stopped at the crosswalk. The red hand blinked away, but the cars were stopped and not going anywhere, so we zigzagged our way around them.

"Because when she mentioned the elevator in Australia, she had a look. I don't know. I can't explain it. I think we should tell her, Zoe. We should tell her everything."

We reached the top of the stairs to the subway. "Everything? You want to tell her about the Badger brothers, how they're after you, and that we left them hanging off the Golden Gate Bridge in 1935? Oh, yeah, and let's tell her all about the time we traveled halfway around the world to India. I'm sure she won't mind."

"Mom had the token before us. She knows how it works."

"Do *you* know how it works, Arcade?"

I reached for the token inside my shirt. "Of course not."

"Then she probably doesn't either. I think we should wait a little longer before we talk to her. We need patience, remember?"

"No, *you* need patience. I need compas—"

Right then something ran into me. Something huge.

"AHHHHHHHHHH!"

I launched into the air like a flying squirrel, totally missing the last few steps, and landed at the bottom of the stairwell, flat on my face. My glasses flew off my face as my chin hit the ground.

"ARCADE!" Zoe's voice echoed through the subway station.

"Oh . . . uh . . . haha . . . sorry!" was all I heard. And then a bunch of laughter and the pounding of feet on concrete as they ran away.

"Hey!" Zoe yelled. "Get back here and apologize, you big . . . ugly . . . SACK OF POTATOES!"

The laughter faded into the distance.

Zoe put her hand on my back. "Arcade, are you all right?"

"Ugggggggh."

"I found your glasses. Here. Thank goodness they're not broken."

I sat up, grabbed the glasses, and jammed them on my face before slowly scooting myself against the wall to make room for the crowds of people passing by. One lady gave me a concerned glance, but I smiled and waved her on.

"Did you notice what *kind of potatoes* hit me?" I tried to smile. "Were they Idaho Russets?"

Zoe wiped a tear from the corner of her eye. "Hey, stop making fun of me when I'm trying to take care of you! He was big. That's all I could see. And his clothes were brown and lumpy. Like a huge potato sack. So that's what came out of my mouth. He had a few other people with him."

"Smaller potatoes? Like tater tots?"

Zoe gently punched me in the arm. "Very funny. I didn't catch any other details. I was busy watching you fly through the air as they ran by."

"Did I look cool at least?"

Zoe scrunched up her mouth. "*Super* cool. For a flying dork."

I rested my face in my hands. "I hope no one had their phones out taking videos."

Zoe put out her hand to pull me up. "I do. Then maybe we could ID those guys. And the video would totally go viral. It was *that* ridiculous."

Still a little woozy, I took a step and kicked my phone across the concrete toward the subway turnstile. I put both arms up in the air. "GOAL!"

Zoe ran and picked it up. She frowned when she looked at it and handed it back to me. "Sorry. Screen's cracked."

"Oh, man! NOT cool." I swiped my finger on the screen. "At least it works. For now."

A subway car rumbled in the distance. "We better go, Arcade. I think that's our train."

I shoved my phone into my back pocket as Zoe and I approached the side-by-side turnstiles. She swiped her metro card and pushed her way through.

I reached for my flamingo backpack to grab my metro card.

Hey, where's my backpack?

"C'mon, Arcade, we need to catch this train so we aren't late for the bus on Eighth!"

"Uh, Zoe, I'm having a little problem."

Zoe threw her head back. "Please, don't tell me you lost your metro card."

"Okay, I won't tell you that."

"Thank heavens."

"But I did lose my backpack."

"WHAT?"

"And *that* had my metro card in it."

Zoe charged back through the emergency doors. "Arcade! This is NOT GOOD!!" She grabbed both my shoulders and looked me in the eyes. "When did you last have it?"

I thought for a minute. "I'm pretty sure it was hanging on my right shoulder when I launched off the subway steps."

Zoe's eyes widened. "Then let's go back and get it!" She grabbed me by the T-shirt and pulled me back to the scene of the belly flop.

No flamingo backpack anywhere.

"I bet THEY took it." Zoe put a hand on her hip and jutted out her chin.

"The potato family?"

"Yes! The big ugly spud and his tater tots! I bet they stole your backpack."

I looked around and tried to remember the events leading up to my fall. I was sure I had my backpack hanging off my right shoulder. I stared up toward the top of the stairs. I felt sick to my stomach. "Zoe, I think you're right! Russet man stole my flamingos!"

"What else did you have in your backpack?"

"Snacks. My metro card. A bottle of water. Hey, good news, at least there were no library books."

"That's a miracle." Zoe wiped her forehead. "Do you have any money in your pockets?"

"Nah. I always count on you for money."

She crossed her arms. "Well, it just so happens that I don't have any with me today, so it looks like we'll be walking home."

"Walking? But that's thirty-eight blocks!" I followed Zoe over to the metro card kiosk, where she swiped her card to find out her balance.

"Great, just like I thought. Only one trip left. I was going to use that for the bus trip home."

"So we're not taking the subway?"

"Not unless your Triple T Token can get you in. Wait!" she said, before I could even open my mouth, grabbing my wrist with a nervous smile on her face. "Forget I said that."

"Can we call Mom and Dad?"

Zoe shook her head. "They're at the doctor, remember?"

"Then I guess we'll be seeing quite a bit of New York City today." I wiped some sweat from my forehead. "That should help me with my fun goal at least."

"Arcade, walking thirty-eight blocks is NOT FUN!"

I grinned. "Patience, Zoe, remember?"

CHAPTER 4

A Confusing Way Home

At least when we get to 59th we can walk in the park."

Before we moved to New York, I thought Central Park was the *only* park in the city. I found out it isn't. But it is the biggest. And my favorite.

I looked up at the sign as we crossed through more traffic. "Hey, Zoe, I thought we were on Seventh Avenue. This says Broadway."

We both just stared at the sign for a minute. Zoe scratched her head. "I don't understand. We didn't change streets, did we?" She pulled up the GPS app and held her phone toward the sky. "I don't get it! C'mon, phone, WORK!"

"Not gonna happen, sweetie," a lady said as she brushed by Zoe. "Tall buildings block the signal."

Zoe's shoulders drooped. "I guess we'll walk to the next corner and see where we are."

We walked for a bit, passing theater after theater. "Where's *Manhattan Doors* playing?" That's my dad's show.

Zoe shrugged. "I have no idea. Dad pointed it out to

me once when we were riding in a taxi, but Broadway is a really long street. And it must be crooked or something too, because we can't seem to find our way off it."

We walked a few more blocks, searching for Central Park. I turned around and looked everywhere, trying to find a landmark. "It was a lot easier to see it from the top of the Empire State Building."

After a few more minutes of weaving through the crowd, Zoe stopped and held her hands up in the air. "Finally!" She pointed toward Columbus Circle, one of the main entrances to Central Park. "Hey, I think I see Elijah! Let's go say hi."

Elijah is a young, college age guy from Senegal who works as a pedicab tour guide in Central Park. He's *always* out there, rain or shine. "It's my only source of income, so if I miss a day, I may have to miss a meal," Elijah once told us.

"Well, hello, Miss Zoe and Mr. Arcade! How is the day treating you so far?"

Hmmmm. Where do I start?"

I didn't have to, because Zoe went off. "We were doing just fine until Arcade got run over by a huge kid in the subway and got his backpack stolen—which happened to have his metro card in it—and of course I don't have any extra money with me today, so we're walking all the way to 88th."

"Run over? Stolen? Oh, dear, that is quite unfortunate." Elijah looked me up and down. "Were you hurt?"

My chin still throbbed. "A little, but I'm okay. Just mad right now. That was my favorite backpack *of all time*."

Elijah chuckled with his low voice. "Oh, yes, black with flamingos. Am I right?"

"Yeah, that's the one."

Elijah put a finger to his chin. "I remember thinking that a flamingo is an odd bird."

"That's what makes them so interesting," I said. "Did you know that flamingos turn orange because of the pigment molecules in the food they eat?"

Elijah shook his head. "I did not know that."

"And according to a book I read, they also—"

Zoe reached over and covered my mouth. "We don't have time for this today. We have thirty blocks to walk. And flamingos are pink."

I pushed Zoe's hand away. "They're orange."

"Pink."

"Orange."

Elijah laughed. "I think you are both correct! Would you let me have the honor of taking you home?" Elijah gestured to his pedicab.

Zoe shook her head. "We can't pay you, Elijah, and we don't want to keep you from getting business from someone else."

Elijah put a finger to his lips, then dropped his hand down to cover his heart. "Miss Zoe, if I make money today or if I do not make money today, that is up the Lord. But I would not be able to continue my work day in good conscience if I did not take care of my friends who are in need."

I looked around at all the other bike tour guides as they held clipboards, explaining to potential customers about the different tour packages, hoping to be hired for a job. Today was a beautiful day in Central Park, but a little hot to be walking. A perfect business day for Elijah.

"Are you sure, Elijah? There's a bunch of people around here who look like they have money and need rides."

He raised his eyebrows. "Did I not just explain to you about that? Do not worry, my friend."

"Well, okay." Zoe turned to me. "Come on. The sooner he takes us, the sooner he can come back and pick up some business."

Elijah smiled and jumped up on the bike seat. "I like how your sister thinks."

"Hear that, Arcade? Some people *appreciate* my thoughts." Zoe jumped up into the small carriage and gave me the stink-eye as she sat down. And now I had to go sit by her?

Ugh.

The hot August sun beat down on the back of my neck and, man, was I thirsty!

"We can stop by Bethesda Terrace," Elijah said. "I have a friend there who is a food vendor. He'll give us some free snow cones."

"I'm in!" I jumped in the chariot. I'd sit next to Zoe, the know-it-all, all day if it meant flavored ice on a scorching day like today.

Elijah beamed back at me, but then frowned. "Are you okay, my friend? You look droopy."

"What?" I rested my head on the back of the red bike carriage and closed my eyes. It took me a minute to form words. "I guess I'm . . . just . . . *really baking* in here!" When I opened my eyes, the swirly pattern on the pedicab cover started to spin like a pinwheel.

"Brother, you need some water!" Elijah jumped down off his seat. "I will be right back!"

I held my hand out to stop him. "It's okay . . . I . . . just need . . . my . . . flamingo . . ."

Zoe reached over and shook me. "Arcade, what is happening to you?" She put her hand over my heart and immediately pulled it back like she'd just touched a hot stove. "Hey! That crazy thing is blazing again!"

The Triple T Token had come back to life, *hotter* than ever!

"Uh-oh!" I pulled the token out from under my shirt. The thing was smoking! "I guess we know what's coming next . . ."

"Fan it! Blow on it! Cool it down!" Zoe waved her hands so wildly she shook the bike carriage.

I held the token out from my body.

Glitter swirled up from the floor of Elijah's pedicab carriage. It heated my face, like the sparks from the campfires we used to build in Virginia. The shiny pieces popped and snapped.

"Got any marshmallows?" I asked. Zoe smacked me in the arm.

"I'm not ready for this, and you're delirious from heat. Let's ignore it. Please."

"Zoe. I feel like I'm going to explode! That's a little difficult to ignore! And you know that the doors—"

I didn't have to finish, because the elevator doors materialized right in front of us in the carriage. They were gold, with orange and red flames projecting on them as if they were a movie screen. A golden coin slot popped out of the middle.

"We gotta go," I said to Zoe. "You know we gotta go."

Zoe buried her head in her hands. "Where? Where to *this* time?"

I stood, licked my fingers, and reached for the fiery token. I pulled it off the chain. "I don't know. I never know. But if it works the same way it always does, Elijah won't miss us at all."

Zoe gathered her backpack and stood up. "Ugggggh. I hope there's drinking water where we're going."

I carefully placed the token in the coin slot and jumped back when there was a loud *POP!* The doors opened. A cool breeze from air-conditioning hit our faces. Two large water bottles sat on a small table in the middle of the elevator.

"Hmm. Looks like it heard you, Zoe." I stepped in. My sister followed. I grabbed a water bottle off the table, twisted the cap off, and gulped down the icy water. "Ahhhh. Refreshing."

Zoe reached for her bottle, but as she did, the doors closed, and the elevator lurched, knocking it off the table. And then the car plummeted.

"AHHHHHHHHHHHH! HOLD ON, ARCADE!"

"HOLD ON TO WHAT?" I dropped to the floor. The elevator jerked up and down. Loud noises that sounded like we were in a construction zone assaulted my ear drums. Dust seeped in through the crack between the doors. Zoe and I covered our mouths with our hands.

"Are we going underground?" Zoe's eyes grew wide as the sounds got louder and the jerking grew stronger. She crawled to the back corner of the elevator, bracing herself. "It's getting hot in here, Arcade!"

The elevator shook and shook. More dirt filled the air.

"I've always wanted to dig to China!" I shouted.

Zoe was lying on her back, wiping dirt out of her eyes. Glitter sparks flew out of the elevator vents, but when they came into contact with our skin, they turned to cool water droplets.

"This is DOPE!" I collected some drops in my hand and splashed my face with them.

"This is nothing to be excited about, Arcade." Zoe scowled as she tried to smooth her damp hair. "I better not have to meet any new people looking like this."

The car continued its dig for a few more minutes, and finally came to a stop. The dust and glitter settled on the elevator floor, creating a shimmery sludge.

"I wonder where we are?" I sat up and wiped my glasses with the bottom of my T-shirt.

"I don't know." Zoe stood up and brushed glitter off her knees. "But I bet it's not 88th Street."

CHAPTER 5

Welcome to Beijing

It's a little cooler here. But . . . .

Where is here?

Zoe and I grab our water bottles and step out of the elevator. We're indoors, sort of. There are solid walls on one side, large windows on the other. I can see trees, wooden structures, and rocks on the other side of the windows.

"Looks like some kind of exhibit," Zoe says. She points to some signs on the walls that are filled with artistic symbols. They look Chinese.

A group of dark-haired children rush by us with three adults following close behind. And *they* all look Chinese.

I pump my fist. "YAAASSSSSS! We're in China!"

Zoe puts her finger to her lips. "Shhh. Don't act so surprised. We don't want to look suspicious!"

"We just jackhammered our way here from New York City. Embrace it, Zoe, we *are* suspicious."

Zoe grabs my wrist and pulls me into a corner of the exhibit. "Investigate. But try not to act so . . . so . . ."

"Different?"

"No."

"Excited?"

"No."

"Then what?"

"Try not to act so weird." Zoe shakes her head and walks out in front of me. I follow her, watching out the window at all times. Investigating. We round a corner and see a large group of excited people huddled up against the window, staring out.

Zoe moves in for a closer look, and then jumps back and stuffs the heel of her hand in her mouth. She squeals.

"And *you* just told *me* not to be weird?"

Her eyes are huge. She points. "PANDAS. ARCADE, LOOK AT THE PANDAS."

I turn and look.

"Zoe, those are *giant* pandas."

She takes her hand out of her mouth. "I know that, genius." Then she puts her hand back in and squeals again. "They're exquisite!"

I watch the two giant pandas rolling around and munching greenery. "Yeah, they're definitely fun to watch. But if you ask me, flamingos are much more entertaining."

A bunch of kids in matching school uniforms pass by us. One of the girls drops a paper on the floor. She tries to stop and get it but is bumped by a bigger boy, who rushes her forward. When the stampede disappears, I pick the paper up. It's a map with pictures of animals all over it. There are some Chinese symbols at the top. But there is also some English that indicates our location.

"Where are we?" Zoe crowds in next to me, crunching the map.

"Can't you tell? Look around! We're at the BEIJING ZOO." I search the map for our location and tap my finger near the center. "We're here. At the panda house." A bright blotch of color on the map catches my eye. I trace a line with my finger from the picture of the panda to the blotch.

"The flamingos aren't far from here. Looks like they have them in an enclosed aviary."

Zoe rips the paper from my hand. "Why do you need to see flamingos in *China*? You can see flamingos in any zoo. You can't always see giant pandas!"

I stare right at her. "I like flamingos better. Plus, I have a feeling I'm supposed to be there."

I don't wait for Zoe to give permission. I pull the map out of her hands and follow the directions out of the panda house.

Zoe sighs. "Okay, but then we're coming right back here!" She reaches in her backpack for her phone and attempts to take a picture of one of the pandas. She shakes it and then shoves it in her shorts pocket. "My phone never works on these Triple T adventures. Ugh!"

The door to the aviary has a sign on it with Chinese symbols I can't read.

Oh, well. I know what's in here.

I reach for the handle and pull the heavy thing open. A

family enters in behind me and Zoe. When the teenager at the end of the line doesn't close the door all the way, her dad shouts, points to the sign, and pulls the door shut.

"Come on, Zoe, this way!" I follow a sign with an arrow that shows a picture of an orange bird with a crooked beak and very long, uncoordinated-looking legs.

We turn the corner . . . and there they are.

"Look, Zoe! A flamboyance of flamingos." I jostle her with my elbow.

She rolls her eyes. "You mean a flock of flamingos."

"The technical term is *flamboyance*."

"I didn't know you were into technical terms."

"I am when they suit the situation. These birds are show offs. Totally flamboyant. Can't you see that?"

Zoe tilts her head while watching. "You should know." Then she points to a few smaller white ones hanging out by the water's edge. "The young ones are fascinating."

"Yep. They get their color around one year old. They're not as flamboyant yet."

Zoe looks up into the trees in the aviary and grins. "Okay, this *is* pretty cool. I bet there are some birds here that we can't see at home. But I wonder why the token brought us here?"

"Who knows?" I think a minute. "Hey, Zoe, did I just daydream this, or did I say the word flamingo right before the token caught fire?"

Zoe's eyes shift right, left, then down. "Yeah, you did. You weren't making sense. I thought you were about to faint."

"I *was* going to faint. The canopy was spinning, and my thoughts were all mushy. I don't know why I said flamingo."

"You were probably thinking about your backpack."

"I was."

We listen for a few seconds as some of the flamingos squawk and march around with their necks stretched out.

"Hey, Zoe . . ."

"Yeah?"

"Do you think that—"

"What?"

"Do you think that maybe I controlled the token this time? I mean, I said the word flamingo, and here we are."

Zoe turns toward me, grabs both my shoulders, and shudders. "Lord help us if you start controlling the token."

I pull her hands off me. "Why? What would be wrong with that? I'd take us to some great places if I were in control."

"Hey!" Zoe points toward one of the young, white flamingos trotting over to the water's edge. It hops up on the trail and starts walking—fast.

"Whoa! That's an adventurous one. I've never seen a flamingo leave its flock before."

"You mean, it's *flamboyance*, don't you, Arcade?"

"Hey, he's really moving out! Let's follow him! Come here, little guy! You're supposed to be wading in this water over here!"

The little white flamingo flaps its wings and picks up speed toward the exit to the aviary, just as the family with the teenager decides to leave. The dad is in the front of the line this time, so he doesn't notice the teenager leaving the door propped open. Again!

"Oh, no! It's moving toward the open door! Hurry up, Zoe!" We pick up the pace.

"Hey, flamingo! Flamey! Flames! Get back here! Don't follow them!" I yell, but the determined flamingo charges for the door. "ESCAAAAAAAPPPE!" I yell at the top of my lungs and have visions of the little flamingo running into another exhibit and getting eaten by a tiger or crushed under an elephant's foot.

The awkward bird shoots out the door. Then he takes a few running steps, flaps his wings, and begins to fly low to the ground.

"Catch him, Arcade!" Zoe and I run down the pathway after the flamingo, who finally tires and lands near a bench. I kick into high gear, and as I come closer, he turns to me, and lets out a loud, high-pitched, *SQUAWK*!

I laugh and grab him up in my arms. "Flames, you gotta get back into the bird house. There are wild animals out here." I have never held a flamingo, and I hope he won't try to take a chunk out of my nose with his beak.

Zoe catches up to us, breathing hard. "Unbelievable, Arcade! Leave it to you to go on a bird chase in China." She stops for a minute and pets the flamingo's soft, white feathers.

SQUAWK!!!!!

Zoe pulls her hand away and steps back. "Hey, don't complain to me, bird. You're the one who escaped your home." Zoe looks around. "We better put him back, Arcade."

A few curious kids surround us, and I have to push through

them to get back on the path to the aviary. They reach out to pet the flamingo, but I pull him in tight and shake my head. "He's trembling. We have to get him back to his house."

Suddenly, I hear a deep voice, yelling something in Chinese. Zoe's eyes widen as she points behind me. I turn my head to see three adults in zookeeper uniforms, jogging toward me.

"Oh, man, we're busted!!" I run toward the doors of the aviary, which now look like they're on fire. Swirling, snapping pieces of orange and red glitter rise up from the ground. I swallow hard.

"NOOOOOOO! Not NOW! I have to get this little guy back . . ."

I feel a clunk on my chest. The Triple T Token has returned. I pick up speed toward the door. The zookeepers' shouts are louder now. I consider turning around and trying to explain, but *what* would I say? I don't speak Chinese! By the time I reach the door to the aviary, a mini tornado of glitter is blocking the entrance. A golden coin slot pokes out through the storm.

"Zoe! The token is calling us back!" The flamingo squawks and hooks his neck around my upper arm, like he's trying to hang on.

"Arcade! See if you can open the aviary door and throw him in!" Zoe, who is now standing next to me covered in swirling glitter, gestures toward the door.

I reach out as far as I can, but my hand runs into a different kind of door. Golden elevator doors. The coin slot pulses, and the token singes my skin.

"Ouch!" I pull the token from under my shirt with my free hand. "I'm sorry, Flames, I gotta go." I look into the flamingo's eyes and, for a second, I think he understands me. "As soon as someone opens the door, you fly in and get back to your family, okay?"

I put him down on the ground, and he's immediately covered in glitter. "Take care, adventurous one," I say. I grab the token and it comes off in my hand, just like all the other times.

"Zoe! Are you here?" I can't see a thing because my glasses are plastered with orange and red glitter. She grabs my hand.

"YES. Let's go, Arcade! NOW!!!"

I reach out and move my hand around until it bumps into the slot. I drop the token in and the doors, which are now right in front of the aviary, open.

"Hold on!"

Zoe tumbles into the elevator and stays balled up on the ground. I do the same as the doors close and the elevator begins its jack-hammering—UP this time!

It's a shaky ride. Dusty too. Thankfully the air conditioning is going again, and another pair of icy-cold water bottles rolls around on the floor.

Several minutes later, when the dust finally clears, we're sitting back in Elijah's pedicab in Central Park. I recognize him in the distance, purchasing some water bottles from a street vendor. I breathe a sigh of relief, knowing that soon we'll be relaxing in our brownstone on 88th Street.

But then I hear it.

Squawk! Squawk!

We have a stowaway. All the way from the Beijing Zoo.

CHAPTER 6

Squawking Bike

Zoe jumped up off the pedicab seat. "Arcade! What was that noise?"

I looked down at my feet. *Gulp.* Flames the flamingo had his little fluffy neck wrapped around my calf.

"Ummmm . . . that was the sound of this flamingo." I lifted up my foot to show Zoe.

She grabbed her head with her hands. "NO! No, no, no, no, no! This can't be happening. We don't bring things back! That's not how it works!"

I held a finger up in the air. "Well, there was that one time, after the rodeo, when I found your clown nose in the side pocket of your backpack."

Zoe closed her eyes while rubbing both her temples. "A squishy red clown nose is NOT a live flamingo!"

I reached down and smoothed the little guy's feathers. He was shaking, holding on tight to me with his neck. He was still covered with orange glitter, making him look like a grown up, more flamboyant flamingo.

"Aww, he must be so scared. That elevator ride was

really bumpy this time." I reached down, pried him off my leg, and set him on my lap. "It's okay, buddy. I got you."

By this time, Elijah was making his way back to the pedicab with the water bottles.

"Arcade, you have to hide him!" Zoe pulled her backpack off her shoulder and unzipped it. "Put him in here."

I looked in the black hole filled with Zoe's girl things. "But it's hot in there. And he won't be able to breathe with all your perfumed lotions."

Zoe shook her backpack at me. "He's a *tropical* bird. He'll be fine! And we'll leave the top unzipped." She glanced over at Elijah, who was now talking to another pedicab tour guide. "Hurry! It's probably against the law or something to have a flamingo in New York City!"

I took the trembling bird in my hands. "Okay, Flames, this will just be for a little while. Try to stay quiet." I put my finger to my lips and looked in his eyes. "I got you." Then I lifted him up and placed him feet first in the backpack. I set it on the floor of the cab. "Hang in there, adventurous one. You're about to go for a ride through Central Park."

"This will cool you off." Elijah held out a cold water bottle to both me and Zoe. He dried his wet hands on his pants, and then jumped on his pedicab bike seat.

"And now, we go for the snow cones." He turned the handlebars and began pedaling north on the trail toward Bethesda Terrace.

I cracked open the water bottle and took a sip.

Squawk!

Elijah jumped and turned around. I pretended to choke on my water and threw in a snort and a burp to cover for Flames.

"Is everything okay, Mr. Arcade? You sounded like a taxi cab horn just now."

I laughed nervously. "Yes, I'm fine." I coughed and burped again, just for effect.

Zoe slapped me on the back. "Please, excuse my brother. He gulps when he drinks, takes in too much air, and then . . . well . . . you know. The burping around our house can be deafening."

Elijah laughed. I glanced down at Flames. The backpack was rocking gently, and he looked pretty comfortable in it. I reached down and patted his head.

"Elijah," Zoe said, "would it be okay if we took a rain check on the snow cones? It was a very nice offer, but we're really tired, and this water is cooling us down just fine."

Elijah turned left on the path. "Of course, Miss Zoe. I am happy to take you straight home. The flavored ice will be there for a few more weeks, and then we will require hot chocolate to get through the chilly fall and freezing winter days." Elijah popped up off his seat and pumped hard on the pedals to make it up a slight hill going toward our neighborhood. By the time he got to the top, he was breathing hard.

"Which season do you like the best here for biking, Elijah?" I couldn't imagine pedaling people around the park in hot *or* cold weather.

Elijah thought for a long while before answering.
"Every season has its challenges. The summer can be too
hot, the winter terribly cold. The fall is windy, so it fights
me on the bike, and in the spring, well, that is terrible
allergy season for me."

"So you hate them all?"

Elijah shook his head. "No. Actually, I love them all."

"Really? But you just said—"

"No season is perfect for biking. But they are all good
for meeting people and for making a living. There is
something good to be gained in every trial, you know."

I took some more sips from my water bottle and checked
on Flames. He looked like he was asleep, for now.

What am I going to do with this bird?

"Elijah," I said, "have you ever done much exploring in
the Ramble?"

Elijah nodded. "On days when I need a break from
pedaling, I go there to think."

"To think? About birds?" Zoe reached down to steady
her backpack.

Elijah kept his feet moving on the pedals. "Not about
birds. Mostly about how my life is going. How I am
thankful to be here, even though it is not always easy.
Sitting on the benches, looking up at the trees and blue sky,
helps me to focus on what is truly important."

Zoe leaned forward. "And what is that?"

Elijah turned his head to look back at her. "Breathing.
Laughing. Loving people. And lots of other things that I am
still thinking about."

Zoe leaned back and took a deep breath. "I'd like to spend some more time in the Ramble this year. I read there's a secret cave that's not open to the public anymore. Do you know how to get to it, Elijah?"

"Oh, yes. I know where it is."

"Really? Where?" I sat up, ready for Elijah to tell us the location of the cave.

Maybe I could hide Flames there.

But he just laughed. "You'll have to find that yourself, Mr. Arcade. Something tells me that you are not afraid to take part in an adventure or two."

I reached for my chest and covered the Triple T Token with my hand. Thankfully, it was the same temperature as my body, for now.

Zoe and I relaxed for the next few minutes in the back of the pedicab. Someone called Elijah, so he talked on his phone as he pedaled away. I watched as the blocks went by . . . 72nd . . . 73rd . . . 74th . . . this was sure faster than walking.

"Is 85th close enough? That's a natural exit from the park."

"It's great!" I reached down and poked Flames's sleeping head further down in the backpack, stood up, and swung the straps over one shoulder. "I'll get this for you, sis. You look droopy."

Zoe narrowed her eyes and grabbed both water bottles. "Thanks so much, Elijah. You saved us today."

He jumped down off his bike and bowed. "It was my honor and privilege, young lady."

Zoe smiled. "I pray you get lots of business this afternoon to make up for our free ride."

Elijah jumped back on his bike and turned the pedicab around. "Whether I do, or whether I do not, that is up to the Lord. He's got me."

Elijah waved, and we waved back. And just as he was pedaling away, Flames poked his beak out.

Zoe smiled at the bird, then frowned at me. "Seriously, Arcade, what are we going to do with a flamingo?"

I gave Zoe a tight grin. "Not sure. But we'll think of something. Maybe Doug can hide him at his place."

CHAPTER 7

Greenstone for Sale

I love our street!" Zoe tilted her face to the sky and put her arms out, twirling around and around. I love it too. The trees on our street provide great shade in the hot afternoon.

"Okay, let's go see Doug. Maybe Flames can hang out in his extra bathroom."

Zoe and I approached the stairs to Doug's house. "Here we are. My favorite greenstone!"

"It's a *brownstone*, Arcade. How many times do we have to debate this?"

I pointed to the paint on the door. "As many times as we need to until you admit this is green."

Zoe put a hand on her hip. "I know the color is green, but these houses are historically called brownstones."

"HEY, GUYS!" Doug flung the door open and stepped out on the landing. He was munching Chili Cheese Fritos. He's always munching on something, though with his new braces, he's had to cut back on his favorite sticky foods, like gummy bears.

Squawk! Squawk!

Doug dropped the Frito bag. "Whatcha got in that backpack? A bird? Is it Milo?" Milo is my sister's dumb cockatoo that mocks my every word.

"No way, bro! You think I'd take Milo for a walk?" I set the backpack down on the ground. "Is your grandma home?"

Doug glanced back toward the house. "Nah. She's uh . . . getting some special medical care."

SQUAWK!

I unzipped the backpack and pulled Flames out.

Doug jumped back. "WHAT IS THAT?"

I bobbled the bird a bit, but then got him comfortable in my arms. I glanced over at Doug's bedroom window and noticed it had a new sign in it. I pointed to it with my free hand. "WHAT IS THAT?"

"WHAT IS THAT?"

Zoe palmed her forehead. "Here we go . . ."

Doug likes to repeat things people say. It's funny . . . until it's not.

Doug turned to look at the sign. "You answer my question first! WHAT IS THAT?" He pointed to Flames again.

I adjusted Flames some more.

Squawk!

"Dude, this is a flamingo. Can't you tell?"

"Can't I tell?"

"That's what I said."

Doug came in closer to pet Flames. "Aren't flamingos supposed to be orange?"

"Zoe says they're pink."

Doug scrunched up his nose. "Pink? Nah. That's just the fakey plastic ones in Florida."

"Oh, puhleeeeeeze!" Zoe growled. "Must we go over the finer points of flamingos out here where people are bound to walk by and see him?"

"Did you steal him from the zoo?"

"I wouldn't exactly say we stole him. He just sorta hitched a ride with us in an elevator at the Beijing Zoo."

"Beijing Zoo?!?" Doug grabbed my forearm and pulled me into the house. Zoe followed. "Have you been travelin' with that token again?"

I set Flames down on the area rug in Doug's living room, handed Zoe her backpack, and took a seat on the couch.

"Ewwwww. Arcade! He did his business in my backpack!" Zoe dropped it on the floor and covered her face with her hands.

I tried not to laugh. Actually, no, I didn't. I laughed out loud. "Well, he's just a little guy. And at least you *have* a backpack."

"What happened to *your* backpack, Arcade?" Doug sat down on the floor and reached out to pet Flames.

"It was stolen by a sack of potatoes at the entrance to the subway right before Arcade belly flopped down the stairs," Zoe said.

"And we thought we'd have to walk all the way home, but when we reached the park, Elijah gave us a ride in his pedicab. Well, right after we took a little trip through the earth and ended up at the Beijing Zoo."

Doug put both hands on his forehead. "THROUGH the earth? To the Beijing Zoo?"

"That's what I said, Doug."

"Aww, man, you've been goin' to all kinds of crazy places since you got that token. My favorite was my time on Food TV, though."

Doug was the first of my friends to accompany me and Zoe on one of our token adventures. He ended up on a food show called *The Munch*, and was about to make a spectacle of himself, when the token returned us to our regularly scheduled school day—filled with bullies and a nearly impossible year-end assignment from our teacher, Mr. Dooley.

I put my hand over the token. "Yeah, this little token is full of surprises." It heated up just a bit. "But I think—"

"What?" Zoe got a concerned look on her face.

"I think it's changing somehow. The lady on the top of the Empire State Building told me things were about to heat up . . . to test my metal. I don't get what she meant by that."

"The *lady*?" Zoe stood up and started pacing. "The one who gave you the token in the library? You saw her *again*? You didn't tell me she was up there."

"I didn't have time! Mom and Dad showed up and then . . . well . . . we've been a little busy digging through the earth and back."

"But that was IMPORTANT, Arcade! The woman could have given us some answers!"

I shook my head. "She said there was no time for answers. And just that—"

"WHAT?"

"That things were going to heat up to test my metal. And it's part of the process. *And* I'm supposed to trust the tester." I scratched my head. "What's a tester?"

Zoe picked up a couch pillow and threw it at me. "YOU SHOULD HAVE ASKED HER."

Squawk!

Flames ran over and pecked Zoe on the ankle.

"OUCH!!!! Why did you do that?"

I laughed. "Looks like he's protecting me."

"But I'm the one who gave him my backpack to use as a bathroom."

Squawk!

"Is that *really* a flamingo?" Doug examined Flames's feathers. "Why isn't he orange?"

"Flamingos are pink," Zoe said.

Ugh. Time to change the subject.

"Hey, Doug, what was that sign in your front window?"

Doug settled back on his hands on the floor. "Oh, that." He sighed. "It's a For Sale sign."

I sat up straight. "Is your greenstone for sale?"

"Brownstone," Zoe said.

I ignored Zoe and looked back at Doug. "Well, IS IT?"

Doug stood up and then *he* began pacing. "Yeah, Arcade. I didn't know how to tell you but . . . the greenstone is for sale."

I walked right up and put my face in front of his. "But WHY? Your grandma's lived here all her life. Where does she want to go? Where could you go that would be better than here?"

Doug grabbed his bag of Fritos from the couch. He frantically munched, and chili-cheese crumbs fell to the floor.

"It's like this. Grandma's not doing so good. She doesn't want to move from here, but she . . . I mean . . . I . . . well . . . *we* can't take care of her anymore. She has to go to an assisted living place, and she needs the money from the sale of this place to pay for it."

Zoe and I just stared at Doug. Flames stopped his exploring and stared at Doug too.

Doug continued, "Okay. She's sort of *already* in an assisted living place."

"Sort of?" Zoe walked over and put a hand on Doug's shoulder.

Doug slumped a little. "Yeah. She's been there two weeks."

"Doug," I walked over and pulled the chip bag out of his hands. "Why didn't you tell us? Have you been staying here alone for two weeks?"

Doug nodded. "I figured if I told you, that would mean that it's really happening, and I *really* don't want this to happen."

A knot formed in my throat. I didn't know what to say.

"And then that lady realtor came by today and asked to put up the sign. Do you think anyone's gonna want to buy this place?"

We all looked around at the cozy home, with the new wood flooring and light-blue painted walls covered with watercolor paintings of Central Park. My favorite thing was the built-in fireplace in the corner. Doug and I had spent plenty of time sitting in front of it last spring trying to figure out how to survive with bullies Kevin and Casey Tolley living on our block.

Zoe nodded. "Yep. This place is gonna sell fast."

We all sat silently for a few seconds. My mind filled with more questions. "Doug, where are you going to live? Can you stay with your grandma?"

Doug shook his head. "Nah. It's against the rules."

"So what are you supposed to do?" I held both hands toward the ceiling.

Doug took a deep breath. "I don't know. I've got a social worker coming over in a couple weeks to help me figure that out."

"Social worker? A couple *weeks*?" Zoe gave me a side glance.

Doug held his hand out and I handed back his Frito bag. He dug in, but just came up with crumbs. "Yeah. I guess since I'm only eleven-and-a-half they won't let me live on my own. I think they're going to put me in foster care."

"Doug," Zoe said, "how old is your grandma?"

"Eighty-seven. She's actually my great-grandma. My grandma died before I was born."

"Oh, Doug. I'm so sorry."

Doug licked his Frito fingers. "Thanks."

"And where are your parents?"

"ZOE!"

Doug put a hand out. "It's okay, Arcade. The answer is, I don't know. I just know that they haven't been acting like parents for a long time."

"But . . . foster care?" I gulped. "Where? With who?"

Doug flopped down on the big brown chair in the corner of the room. "Don't know. Whoever wants to take a hyper preteen boy who devours large quantities of food, I guess."

Doug sat there, staring at the ceiling. Finally, he got up and spoke. "What are you going to do with Flames? Keep him at your house?"

"Nah. If we did that we'd have to explain where he came from to my parents, and I don't even know how I'd begin to tell them about the token."

Doug's eyes lit up. "You wanna keep him here for now? I mean, until I have to move?"

SQUAWK! SQUAWK! SQUAWK!

I ran over and sat down next to Flames. "Flames, you gotta keep quiet. Everyone in the neighborhood will hear you."

Doug grabbed his stomach. "You know what? I think he might be hungry." He took a few Frito crumbs in his hand and held them out for Flames. Flames pecked for a minute but decided chili cheese wasn't his flavor.

"Of course!" I said. "Who knows when he last ate."

"So, Mr. Flamingo Expert," Zoe said, "what do flamingos eat?"

"Shrimp. I read that in a library book. You got any shrimp, Doug?"

Doug jumped up and raised his hands in the air. "Have I got any shrimp? People don't call me the Food Dude for nothin'!"

I cracked up. "Doug, *nobody* calls you the Food Dude."

"Oh, yeah. That's just what I call myself sometimes when I'm cooking. Anyways, follow me into the kitchen, friends. I was planning to sauté me up a little shrimp carbonara later in the week, but I suppose I could share some with our little flamingo."

SQUAWK!

We made our way into the kitchen, and Doug pulled a five-pound bag of shrimp out of the freezer! He filled the sink with water and dumped in the bag of shrimp.

"Flamesy, you're one lucky flamingo! You ended up in the Food Dude's kitchen! And you're about to have some nice, raw shrimp carbonara, minus the carbonara!" Doug swirled the bag around in the warm water. "Hey, Arcade, you ever wonder why shrimp isn't orange till you cook it?"

Zoe shook her head. "Shrimp is pink."

I threw my hands up. "Seriously, Zoe? Your nose is pink!"

After Flames demolished his raw shrimp dinner, we took him upstairs to get him settled in Doug's extra bathroom.

"He can't get into too much trouble up here," Doug said. "Should we fill up the bathtub a little? You know how those flamingos like to splash around at the Bronx Zoo."

"Actually, I've never been there. That's a goal of mine this year. To see New York stuff. But hey, I *have* been to the Beijing Zoo."

"Man, I wish I could have been with you guys when you went there. Do you think I'll ever get to go on another Arcade adventure? They're the best!"

I glanced down at my chest. There was sizzling happening under my shirt, and I had a feeling it wasn't heartburn.

"Why are you sweating?" Doug laughed as he filled the bathtub for Flames. Zoe jumped up from the little footstool where she had been sitting, feeding dessert shrimp to Flames.

"Arcade, is your token acting up again? Please tell me you're sweating because you forgot to use deodorant today."

"Zoe, my face is sweating. I don't put deodorant on my face!" The token jumped off my chest, and then dropped. When it dropped, it sizzled.

"I don't understand," I said to the token. "Can you help me understand? Where did you come from?" I placed the token between both hands and wished to know.

CHAPTER 8

Squawks and Sparks

Flames squawked and kicked water in the bathtub with his webbed feet, and Doug's bathroom suddenly filled with sparking orange glitter. It sprayed out of the wall air freshener that was plugged into an electrical outlet. And the temperature in the small room rose at least ten degrees.

Zoe reached in her pocket and pulled out a hair tie. She gathered her hair up in a ponytail and wiped some sweat off the back of her neck. "WHY does it have to be so HOT?"

"The old lady said things would heat up. In all ways. To test my metal."

"Metal?" Doug asked. "What metal?"

"I haven't figured that out. The only metal I have is this thing around my neck."

Glitter swirled and popped, and the shower doors became golden-colored elevator doors, with a golden coin slot, shaped like a soap dish, poking out of the middle.

Doug stepped in closer to me. "Is that token actual gold? Like, all the way through?" He reached for it, pulled it up to his mouth, and bit it. "Owww! It burned my tongue!"

"Well, why did you put the burning thing in your mouth?"

"I've seen people do that with gold in movies. To test it, to see if it's real. I didn't know it was *that* hot! You sure you don't have a Triple T branded on your chest?"

I panicked and pulled my shirt out to look. "I hope not!"

Then, the token started to spark. And smoke. There was only one thing for me to do. I reached for the token and it came off in my hands. I had to juggle it back and forth to keep it from burning my palms. On about the third juggle, it shot straight into the coin slot.

"Flames, you stay here this time. We'll be right back."

I slapped my palms together and then pulled them apart. The doors opened. Zoe, Doug, and I jumped into a glitter shower that would take us to who-knows-where.

The inside of the elevator was cool, like on our trip to the zoo. But this time it was a smooth ride. And dead quiet. I started humming to break the silence—and the tension—in the air.

"This is eerie." Zoe walked slowly around the elevator, smoothing her hands against the walls. "I can hear my heart pounding."

"I sure hope we're not going up," Doug whimpered.

Doug's been with me on a couple really high adventures, once to the top of an Egyptian pyramid, and then to the year 1935, to the middle of the Golden Gate Bridge before it was completed on both sides. That one was the scariest of all. We escaped into the elevator just as the Badger brothers, the two guys who will do anything to get my token, flew off the edge of the bridge and into the fog.

"Doug, I think I can hear your heart pounding too," Zoe said.

Finally, after another few minutes of deafening silence, the doors opened.

We're in some kind of tall office building, like the Empire State Building. A sign in front of us says that we've landed on the twenty-third floor. Another sign stands next to it. It looks like a kid painted it with gold glitter. It says *Tested and True Gold Refinery* with an arrow pointing right.

"Well, this is better than being stuck on an unfinished bridge in the fog!" Doug steps out of the elevator. "You think they have a snack bar anywhere?"

Zoe goes out next, but I lag for just a second. I have a funny feeling about this place, and for the first time since I started these adventures, I don't want to go.

Zoe turns back to me. "What's wrong?"

I stay in place. "What do you think would happen if I don't leave this elevator?" My hands are shaking as I grab my empty gold chain.

Zoe comes back in and stands by me for a minute. She puts her hand on my shoulder. "Well . . . let's see . . . what do you think would happen if you never opened another library book?"

I shudder. "I guess I would stop learning new things."

"Would you say that these elevator doors are taking us places where we're learning new things?"

I take a deep breath. "Yeah. And each place we've been, I've been able to help another person with what I learned."

"So why won't you step out today?"

My legs feel weak. "Because I think this lesson is for me."

Zoe turns to me and crosses her arms. "Well, then don't you think this is the most important one?"

I look down at the ground. I can't answer. I see Zoe extend her hand.

"C'mon. I got your back."

CHAPTER 9

Pure Gold

There are gold arrows on the floor that I guess we're supposed to follow. No one is in the hallways. Just me, Zoe, and Doug. I search for clues about what city we're in. Or state. Or country. But there are just those golden arrows. Finally, after walking in circles through hallways that seem to go nowhere, we come to a door. It says TEST ROOM.

"What do you want to do, Arcade?" Zoe grabs my hand again. Doug is behind me, close. I can feel his breath on my neck.

I stand there for a minute to think.

What do I want to do? I want to run back to the elevator.

I look at Zoe, then Doug, then back at Zoe. They're waiting for my decision.

Trust the tester . . .

"Let's go in." I reach for the door handle but, as I do, the door opens by itself.

"Arcade, what is this place?" Doug whispers as we look inside.

"It's a warehouse, I guess."

I really don't know for sure what we're looking at. Adults wearing white coats stand beside huge, steaming vats. I watch the guy closest to us pull a flaming orange container out of his vat and carry it over to a large work table. He pours glowing liquid into a dark metal container. When he is finished, he looks up, right at us! But then he goes back to his vat.

"Dude, do you think we're *invisible*?" Doug is examining his outstretched arms.

"Either that, or the guy is very nearsighted. Like me." I adjust my glasses on my face.

"Or he's ignoring us for some reason," Zoe says. "C'mon."

Another guy brings his flaming container over to the same work table. "Not much here. Just a few flakes. A lot of scrap." He pours a small amount of liquid into the dark container.

"That's too bad," a woman standing next to him says. "I had high hopes for that one."

Wait a minute . . .

I take a few steps closer. I can barely believe my eyes.

Is that the woman who gave me the token?

It looks like her, but she's not wearing her regular white sweat suit and Triple T ball cap. She's wearing a white coat, like all the other workers in the room, and her hair is tucked up into a gold bandana.

I elbow Zoe. "Zoe, what does the patch say on her coat?" Zoe's farsighted, so she needs reading glasses, but she can see distances way better than me.

Zoe takes a half-step closer and cranes her neck forward. "It says Quality Control."

"So she's some kind of inspector, then?"

Zoe shrugs. "I guess so."

"I'm gonna test my invisibility," Doug proclaims, and he struts right up to a vat in the middle of the room.

DOUG!

Workers walk around him, and he grins back at us, waving his hands in the air.

"They can't see us." Zoe has to grab the sleeve of my T-shirt to move me forward. "Let's follow the Quality Control woman."

She is walking from vat to vat, staring into the steaming fires. Zoe and I stay a few feet behind her.

"This one is all scrap," a man says, as he carries his container to pour the contents out at the work table.

The woman yells out to the workers, "Keep testing! One of these will come out pure."

"Guys! Check it out!" Doug motions us over to a table at the far corner of the huge warehouse. We jog over, dodging workers along the way.

"We got gold bars, people!" Doug reaches over, pulls a gold bar off the table, and hands it to me. "Of course, I'd prefer a chocolate bar . . . or an ice cream bar. But gold is pretty awesome too."

I take the bar from Doug and turn it over to examine it. It's gold all right. It has words and numbers stamped into it. 100 grams. 999.9 Fine Gold.

"999.9? What's that mean?"

Zoe takes the bar from me. "It means this gold is as pure as you can get it. It's scientifically impossible to remove all the impurities."

"That doesn't make sense," I say. "If they know how to get rid of all the *other* impurities, why not just finish the job and get that last speck out?"

Doug takes the bar back from Zoe. "Where do you think that last speck is hiding?"

A loud shout comes from one of the men in the room. "Boss! Come quick!"

The familiar woman with the Quality Control badge rushes over. We follow. "Have you found something?" She wrings her hands.

"We left this one in the fire a little longer. It's registering one-hundred percent. Do you want to test it yourself?"

The woman nods, takes a stick out of her coat pocket, and dunks it in the fiery liquid. She waits, and appears to hold her breath, while something registers on the side of the stick. She gasps. "One-hundred percent. I KNEW it was possible!"

The man holding the handle of the container begins to shake.

The woman puts a calming hand on his arm. "Careful now, follow me to the mold." She leads him to a side door of the big warehouse. She takes a key out of her other coat pocket, unlocks the door, and we all walk in.

"I've been waiting for this for a *long* time," she says. "Go ahead and pour it in."

The man approaches the small table that holds a small, round mold, but stops short of pouring in the liquid. "Are you *sure*? I mean . . . you're gonna waste the power of pure gold on some kid?"

The woman smiles. "It won't go to waste. Not when it finds the right kid."

The man hesitates a moment more. "Okay. You're the boss. You sure it won't spill over in this tiny mold?"

"It will all fit just fine. Pour away."

The man does as he's told. Zoe, Doug, and I watch as the red-hot liquid streams into the mold.

I poke Zoe with my elbow and whisper, "What were you saying about things being scientifically impossible?"

Zoe focuses in on the gold, now forming in the mold.

"Arcade . . ." Zoe's mouth drops open.

"Because if it was scientifically impossible then—"

"Arcade!"

"Stop trying to change the subject, Zoe. When you're wrong you're—"

"ARCADE!" Zoe's eyes are bugging out of her head. She just points at the table, the mold now filled to the top with gold.

"It's . . ."

My heart leaps in my chest and goosebumps form on my arms. "Yeah. I know. It's my Triple T Token."

"And it's looking for the right kid."

Now it's my turn to stand there with my mouth hanging open. I push my glasses up on my nose. "The *right* kid? What does that mean?"

Zoe stares up at me. "One who best matches the token, I think."

"But Zoe, I'm not one-hundred percent pure. I'll never be. It's not possible."

"Ha! How well I know that! You're right, no one is perfect. But the token is. So, what if the token is looking for someone it can trust to use its power perfectly? Maybe *that's* you, Arcade."

The woman and man leave the room, and we follow them out to the steaming warehouse. She dips her stick into a few more containers and shakes her head.

"*Maybe* it's me? How will I know? How will the token know?"

Zoe begins to pace. Her hands are glued to both sides of her head. She closes her eyes, and her face contorts. Then she stops, shakes her head, and takes a deep breath. "Arcade, I don't know how to tell you this." She takes another deep breath.

"I know what you're going to say."

"This is totally out of the box for me."

"I know."

"And it wouldn't make any sense, except that . . . we're here, and that doesn't make any sense either."

Silence. Zoe gathers herself.

"Arcade, the only way the token will know if you'll

use it properly is to put you through the fire, just like *it* just went through the fire."

Gulp.

"And now," she says with a sympathetic smile, "I know why you were afraid to get out of the elevator."

This whole time Doug has been standing there with his mouth hanging open. "Zoe, what are you saying?"

"The woman on top of the Empire State Building said that things were about to heat up, right? To test your metal?"

"Yeah," I say. "That still doesn't make sense."

"Arcade, I don't think she meant the word metal, m-e-t-a-l. I think she was referring to the word mettle, m-e-t-t-l-e. It means strength of character, courage, determination, the ability to cope in the midst of difficult circumstances."

"Difficult circumstances?" The knot in my throat returns.

Zoe puts both hands on my shoulders. "Arcade, I think that Triple T Token hanging around your neck is a fiery 'mettle' tester—"

I look down. And there it is, back on the chain.

". . . and it's about to test *you.*"

The fiery metal tester pulses light.

"It's time to go." I pull the warehouse door open and we

exit back into the hallway. The gold arrows have switched direction!

We follow them back to the elevator doors, where glitter is rising up and the golden coin slot is waiting.

I stall.

"Now what?" Zoe asks.

"Now I'm afraid to go back! What's going to happen? What will the tests be? Will I pass, or will I turn out like the Badger brothers? What if I'm NOT the right kid?"

Zoe puts her hand on her hip. "You ask too many questions."

"Hey, Arcade?" Doug rubs his belly. "Can we get some food?"

"Sure, Doug." I chuckle and grasp the token between my palms. "We *need* food." Then I pull it off the chain and drop it into the golden coin slot.

CHAPTER 10

Shrimp Break

When we stepped out of the elevator, I expected to see Flames splashing and squawking in Doug's bathroom. But this time was different.

We were standing in a fish market.

"Yes! Arcade, you did it! Cha-ching! Early dinner time."

Zoe's jaw hung open. Mine too. Usually the token takes us right back where we started.

"Please tell me we're in New York City." I backed out of the market and checked the sign. *Empire Fish Market*. I recognized the familiar New York City skyscrapers with scaffolding surrounding them. "Whew!" I walked down to the corner to check for street signs. "OH, NO!" Zoe and Doug caught up to me, and they both looked up. Waaaaay up.

"Hey, isn't that the Empire State Building?" Doug laughed.

"Right back where we started!" Zoe stomped her foot and pounded her legs with her fists.

"And now *neither one* of us has a backpack," I said.

"Or money," Zoe added.

"Money? You need money?" Doug was still gawking at the Empire State Building. "I got money."

"You do?" Zoe blew out a breath. "Good. How much?"

Doug reached into his shorts pockets and pulled out three crumpled, one-dollar bills. "I keep subway money in all my pants, just to be safe. How much do you need?"

Zoe frowned. "Three times that much *if* we all want to ride the subway home."

"What about food?" Doug gulped and patted his stomach.

"Maybe you should use that three bucks for a hot dog," I said.

"LIVINGSTON AND BAKER! HOW NICE TO SEE YOU!"

The booming voice was unmistakable. I had listened to it every school day for the last six weeks of sixth grade. Mr. Dooley. He walked toward us, carrying an Empire Fish Market bag.

"AND YOU ARE ZOE, CORRECT?" Mr. Dooley tipped his newsboy cap toward Zoe.

Zoe smiled. "Yes, we met the day of the career expo. How are you enjoying your summer, Mr. Dooley?"

"OH, SUMMERS ARE GLORIOUS! THIS ONE IS HOT, BUT AT LEAST I'M NOT HAVING TO PUT UP WITH THE SMELL OF SWEATY SIXTH GRADERS IN THE CLASSROOM."

Seriously, I think his voice had gotten louder during the summer!

"AND WHAT BRINGS YOU YOUNG PEOPLE DOWN TO MIDTOWN THIS WARM AUGUST DAY? DID I JUST SEE YOU RUN OUT OF MY BROTHER'S FISH MARKET?"

"Your *brother's* fish market?"

Mr. Dooley nodded. "Yes, Arcade. Patrick Dooley, owner of Empire Fish Market. Come with me. I'll introduce you."

"PATRICK, THIS IS ZOE, DOUG, AND ARCADE. DOUG AND ARCADE ARE MY STUDENTS."

Mr. Dooley pulled a fifty-dollar bill out of his pocket and placed it on the counter. "HOOK THEM UP WITH SOME OF YOUR BEST FISH."

Patrick, a sunny, smiling guy, yelled from behind the fish counter. "Anything for my favorite brother!"

"Wow, thanks Mr. Dooley," I said.

"You are welcome, Arcade. Now you all better get in line. This place will be hopping soon. I have an appointment, so I have to run. BUT I'LL SEE YOU TWO BOYS AT SCHOOL IN ONE WEEK!"

And with that, Mr. Dooley opened the door to the fish market. The little bell jingled, and he was gone.

CHAPTER 11

Boyfriend on Broadway

"Did Mr. Dooley say he'd see us at *school*? Did he forget that we're going to middle school?" I picked up the pace to try to catch Zoe, who was speed walking north, away from the fish market.

Doug put a hand to his forehead and squeezed. "I don't know, Arcade. Maybe we didn't pass the sixth grade and they forgot to tell us."

"Nah, I'm sure we passed."

Zoe stopped and turned to yell back at us. "Pick it up, boys! At this rate, we won't make it home for dinner!"

Doug and I did our best to catch up, but it wasn't quite fair. After all, we were the ones carrying the heavy bags of shrimp.

"You think Mr. Dooley's brother bought our story about why we needed so much shrimp?" Doug lifted the bag up and took a huge whiff.

"Why *wouldn't* he believe us? We have a friend visiting from out of town who lives for shrimp and we want to surprise him. That's the truth!"

"But who's the friend?" Doug asked.

"*Who's* the *friend*?"

"Yeah, who's the friend?"

"Who's splashing around in your bathroom right now?"

"Who's splashing around in my bathroom right now?"

Zoe stopped and threw her hands up in the air. "BROADWAY! Why can't we get off Broadway?"

Doug and I stopped, and I pointed to the street signs at the crossing. "It's 54th and Broadway. We're making progress! We've gone twenty blocks so far."

Zoe gave me the crazy eyes. "We are NOT making progress! Your token is taking us in circles! We were lost on Broadway *two hours ago*, remember?"

"Zoe?"

A young man's voice came from behind me and Doug. Zoe glanced over our shoulders. Her tense face softened immediately.

"Hi, Michael." Zoe smoothed her hair and straightened her ruffled T-shirt.

Michael Tolley.

Michael Tolley is the older brother of bullies Kevin and Casey Tolley, and they happen to live on our street. And though she's never admitted it, Zoe has a huge crush on him.

Michael held a small bouquet of yellow roses. "Hey, you guys." He wiped a drip of sweat from the side of his face, and transferred the roses to the other hand, which he then whipped behind his back.

"Aww, you brought flowers? What a guy!" Leave it to Doug to create more awkwardness than there already was.

"Oh, uh . . . yeah. The flowers. These are for Trista, if I can ever find her." Michael scratched his head. "No matter how many times I come down here, I always seem to get the theaters confused."

"Trista?" Zoe's voice squeaked. I don't blame her throat for getting a little tight talking about Michael's girlfriend.

"Yeah. She got a call back, and today she finds out if she got the part. Can you believe it? She may end up in a musical on Broadway!"

Doug laughed. "That's ironic! All kinds of people are trying to get *on* Broadway. And we're trying to get off!" He slapped his knee. "Do you know the way *off* Broadway?" Doug looked at Michael, but there was no interrupting whatever he and Zoe had going on.

"Wow. That's, um, quite an achievement. When you see Trista, will you tell her I said congratulations?"

Michael nodded. "Will do. I haven't actually seen her in a few weeks. She's been really busy. Her parents are the ones who told me about the callbacks."

One side of Zoe's mouth turned up in a grin. "Well, at least school starts soon. You'll see her every day then."

Michael fiddled with the roses, switching them from hand to hand, wiping his palms on his shorts. "Not if she gets the part. She'll be working every day and getting her schooling on breaks."

The other side of Zoe's mouth turned up. "I never thought about that. Well, I hope she gets the part. Oh—but not so that you can't see her . . . I mean . . . I'm really happy for her. And you. Well, I'm sure you guys will work something out."

This is torture. Save us, Doug!

"Hey, Michael! Can we bum some money off you for the subway? We're sorta stranded with all this shrimp."

NOT THAT WAY, DOUG!

Michael broke eye contact with Zoe and looked down at the Empire Fish Market bags that Doug and I were holding.

"Shrimp, huh?" Michael came a little closer. "Why do you have so much?"

"We've got a friend from out of town who's shrimp crazy. We're gonna surprise him."

DOUG!

"And we sorta spent all our money on the shrimp, so now we gotta walk all the way home."

Michael's eyes widened. "All the way to 88th?" He dug in his front pocket and turned back to Zoe. "You shouldn't have to walk all that way."

Zoe smoothed her hair. "We're fine. Really. Arcade has this weird goal of seeing more of New York City, so this walk will definitely help him."

"It's a thousand degrees out here. Let me help." Michael pulled a twenty-dollar bill out of his pocket and held it out to Zoe.

Zoe pushed it away. "No, I can't let you do that."

Michael shoved the twenty in the hand with the flowers and grabbed Zoe's hand with his other. "I insist." He tried to put the money in Zoe's hand, but the money and the flowers got tangled and bobbled. Everything hit the ground instead. Michael and Zoe bent down at the same time to pick it all up, and they bonked heads.

Finally! Some good entertainment.
Zoe and Michael both
grabbed their foreheads.
"Oh, man, I'm
such a dork." Michael
bent down and picked
up the money and the
flowers.

"No, that was my fault,"
Zoe said.

Michael grinned. "Yes, it
was. You should have taken the money."

Zoe put a hand on her hip. "What? I was just being
polite. You can't fault me for that!"

"I won't, unless you refuse the money." Michael held
out the twenty-dollar bill again.

TAKE. THE. MONEY. ZOE.

Zoe sighed and looked up at the sky. "Okay, but I'm
going to pay you back."

Michael chuckled. "Okay, you can do that by buying me
lunch at school one day. I'll be the one sitting all by myself
while Trista sings herself to stardom on Broadway."

Zoe smiled. "Deal."

Michael blew out a breath and looked at me. "Wow.
Your sister's a stubborn one."

"Oh, man, you don't even know the half—"

Zoe reached out and put her hand over my mouth. "Be
quiet, Arcade."

Michael turned to leave, but he stopped a second and

looked down. In the collision, a rose had broken out of the bouquet and was laying on the ground. He reached down, picked it up, and handed it to Zoe.

"Have a beautiful day," he said, and then he vanished into the crowd of New York City walkers.

I had to jog to catch up with Zoe, who seemed to be running away from something.

"Hey!" I came up beside her. "Some of us are hauling shrimp, you know. Are we headed to the subway?"

Zoe stopped. "Well, that's the plan, Einstein. I didn't just endure the most embarrassing moment of my life to NOT use this twenty to get us home."

I breathed out. "Oh, good. Hey, that Michael's a nice guy, isn't he?" I pointed to the rose, winked at Zoe, and then ran toward the 59th Street subway station. Zoe followed close behind, kicking the back of my shoe every other step.

Doug caught up with us when we had to stop on the corner at 56th. "We goin' to the subway? I can't wait to meet this shrimp-lovin' friend from out of town." He laughed.

"Yeah, I can't wait to see what damage he's done to your bathroom."

8th Street! Finally!" Zoe waved an index finger at me. "You and that token better behave. I have no more patience for walking today."

"Oh, but you want to develop patience, right? Maybe that calls for one more trip up Broadway."

"Here we are!" Doug ran up the steps to his greenstone. "Time for a big 'ole shrimp fry!"

When we got inside, we were met with extreme squawking from the upstairs bathroom. Zoe pinched her nose. "What's that smell?"

Doug sniffed his armpits. "I'm good. Must be Arcade."

I sniffed. "I don't smell anything. Zoe, you have an overactive nose."

"No, I don't. I have an *accurate* nose. Follow me." Zoe started up the stairs, and we followed her to the bathroom door. She sniffed. "There. It's in there." She pulled her T-shirt collar over her nose. "You go first."

Okay, so maybe it did smell a little like seafood—gone bad. I opened the door, then wished I hadn't.

Doug followed close behind. "What's goin' on in Gram's bathroom?"

I stepped aside so he could take a look. Flamingo droppings were *everywhere*, including all over the white rug that Doug's grandma had put down next to the sink.

"I guess we should have moved that out," I said.

"How can *so much* come from that little teeny bird?" Zoe reached down and rolled up the now ruined rug.

"Well, he ate his weight in shrimp before we left," Doug said. "I guess we have to help Flames with a little thing called *portion control*. It had to come out sometime."

Flames flapped his wings and flew into the bathtub. He kicked his webbed feet in the water, throwing a bunch of it up in our faces, like he was showing off.

"Hey, check out his dance!" Doug pulled a towel off the rack and handed it to Zoe, who had caught the biggest splash right in the face. "Looks like the flamenco!" Doug started kicking his feet and snapping his fingers above his head.

Zoe shook her head and dropped her face in the towel. "I'm outta here."

Doug stopped the snapping and looked at me. "Guess she's not into flamenco?"

After cleaning up for half an hour, and then taping garbage bags down on the entire floor of the bathroom, Doug and I made our way down the stairs, exhausted.

Zoe was on the phone with Dad. "How'd the exams go? Oh, that's good. I'm sorry I didn't text when we got home. Yeah, I know. I'm sorry, Dad. We had a few challenges." Zoe glanced up at us. "Can Doug join us for dinner tonight?" She took the phone from her ear and put it on speaker.

"Sure!" Dad said. "We love Doug."

"Can he stay overnight too?" I asked. "He's in a little, uh, situation, and he may need our help. I'll explain later."

"Sure, Arcade. You know he's always welcome here."

Zoe hung up. I followed Doug up to his bedroom to help him pack some clothes, a sleeping bag, and his pillow in a big black garbage bag we had left over from Flames's cleanup.

"I don't have a good feeling about this, Arcade. I don't want to move away from this street, this city, all my friends. Especially you. I mean, I knew Gram was getting older and that someday this would happen, but I'm only eleven-and-a-half. I don't have any closer family than her. Am I gonna end up living out of a bag or box and be homeless?"

"Nah." I swept my hands in the air. "Not gonna happen. I won't let it."

Doug looked down at my chest. "You think your pure gold token can do anything?"

I grabbed it, and it flared heat, but just for a second.

Can I control it? Really?

"Well, one thing's for sure. If I can make this thing find you a home, I will."

CHAPTER 13

Schedule Scare

That night at dinner, we told my parents about Doug's grandma, and how Doug had been staying at his house all by himself for the last two weeks.

Dad shook his head. "That's not acceptable. You can stay with us, Doug. That way you can keep your house clean so that when the realtor wants to show it, you're ready."

"That's a great idea," I said.

Except that the upstairs bathroom is being trashed by a flamingo doing the flamenco.

Loopy, my chocolate-colored shih-poo, climbed up on my lap and couldn't stop sniffing and licking my shirt.

"Loopy! C'mon, man! I know I've been gone all day, but this is ridiculous!" He popped his head up near my chin and licked my mouth.

"Ha!" Doug pointed to some slobber that was tracked on my shirt. "It's almost like he smells another dog, or some other more exotic animal. Hey, Loopy, you like shrimp?"

A loud knock at the front door made me jump. Loopy leapt down and ran over. Dad got up to open it.

"Well, hello, Kevin and Casey. How is everything at the Tolley residence?"

Kevin AND Casey!?! Ugh . . .

Kevin and Casey Tolley are twins. Double-trouble. I can never tell them apart. One of them has a chipped tooth, but I can't remember which one. It doesn't really matter, though, because neither one of them ever smiles anyway.

"Uh, hey, Mr. Livingston." One of them stepped into our house. "Is Arcade here?"

"Yeah, we're lookin' for Arcade," the other one grunted. He was holding a paper in his hands.

Loopy barked and then sneezed twice. He might be allergic to Tolleys.

Dad waved me over to the living room. "Son, you have visitors." As if these were civilized people coming over for tea. "And now, if you'll excuse me, I have to get ready for work."

I grabbed Doug's sleeve and pulled him into the living room with me. "Stay close," I whispered. We went out to meet team Double-Trouble.

"Hey, Kevin, Casey. What's up?"

"What's up?" Doug said.

The Tolley on the left shook his paper in my face. "*This* is what's up. We got another year with Dooley!"

I reached out to take the paper. It was the official MS 230 class schedule for Kevin Tolley. And it said that his homeroom teacher was, sure enough, DOOLEY.

"Hmmmmmm."

"My schedule's the same," Casey said. "We won't survive

another year with Dooley! He never backs down with the homework. You better be in our class to help us, Arcade."

Then he walked up close. We almost bumped noses.

Oh, no, not this again.

"Well? Are you in our class or NOT?" Casey stared into my eyes.

"I, uh . . . I haven't checked email today." I looked over at Doug, and he just shrugged. "I've been a . . . little busy."

Casey backed up and sat down on our couch. "We'll wait while you check it."

"Where's your computer?" Kevin looked around. He spied the laptop on the desk in the corner of the dining room.

Mom peeked out from the kitchen. "Do you need something, Arcade?"

I gulped. "Yeah, Mom. Did my school schedule come in your email today?"

Mom wiped her damp hands on a kitchen towel and walked over to the computer. "I haven't checked yet. But I can now."

The quicker the better. Get these guys out of here.

Mom opened her laptop, typed in her username, and scrolled through her inbox. "Ah, yes! Here it is. Schedule for Arcade Livingston, seventh grader at MS 230. This is so exciting!" Soon enough, the printer on the desk was spitting out my schedule. I walked over, said a silent prayer that I wouldn't be in *any* classes with the Tolleys, and picked up the single sheet of paper that would define my first year in middle school.

The Triple T Token sizzled on my chest. I began to sweat. *This can't be happening.*

Homeroom: DOOLEY

Bad breath settled on the back of my neck. "Well, that's a relief. Guess that means we'll be working together again this year, Arcade." Kevin gave me a sinister grin. "Our pal Wiley Overton is in our class too. He's even more fun than us. Guess you better study up, bookworm. We gotta do good in seventh grade, you know."

At the end of sixth grade, both Kevin and Casey had tried to force me to do their career expo projects for them. Thankfully, I was able to trick them into doing their own, and they actually turned out really great. But that was just one assignment.

How am I going to make it through a whole year with these guys?

Loopy came over and plopped himself at my feet. He barked Casey back a couple of feet.

Good dog. Can you bark them all the way out the door? How about into another school system?

"So, who's Wiley Overton?" I asked. "And what makes him so fun?"

Casey and Kevin made their way to the front door, both chuckling.

"Who's WILEY OVERTON?" one of them said. "He's just the biggest seventh grader you'll ever meet. He got kicked out of PS 23 in the third grade."

Gulp.

"Why'd he get kicked out?"

"Fighting," Casey said, "with just about everyone at school. Ha! You should ask your friend Baker here who Wiley gave a black eye to on Halloween."

I turned to Doug. "Who?"

Doug poked his chest with his thumb. "This guy."

CHAPTER 14

Mail Call

"Arcade, someone sent you some mail!" Zoe nudged me out of my reading trance the next Tuesday afternoon. I was studying a book about the California Gold Rush. Now that I knew I had pure gold hanging around my neck, I was obsessed with knowing where it came from. During the weekend, I had visited the Ivy Park Library, and Ms. Weckles, the children's librarian, hooked me up with several books about gold. And since I had left the Badger brothers "hanging out" back in California, I figured I might as well study about the Golden State first.

I looked up from my book. "Email?"

Zoe laughed and flicked an envelope in my direction. "No. Snail mail."

I sat up from the couch. "Really? Who would send me mail in an envelope?" I reached out to retrieve it from the floor. I read the return address.

Miss Gertrude Badger

Cimarron Road
Forest, Virginia

"That's dope! Miss Gertrude sent me mail!"

"Really?" Zoe zoomed over and plopped down on the couch next to me. "Maybe the Badgers have returned, and she sent a letter to warn you."

Goosebumps covered my arms. "That wouldn't be good at all."

"But you'd want to know, right? If they've returned? So you can keep an eye out for them?"

Doug entered the room with a handful of snacks from our kitchen. "Did someone say Badger? Are they back? Did they survive their fall off the Golden Gate Bridge?" He ran over and shoved himself next to me on the other side of the couch.

"Open it, Arcade," Zoe insisted.

"Yeah, open it, Arcade."

I elbowed them both so I could get some breathing space. I grabbed a small piece of the envelope on the end and ripped down.

"That's not how you open mail," Zoe said. "You're supposed to turn it over, and loosen the triangular flap—"

I elbowed her again. "I'm eleven, Zoe. I use technology. Give me some beginner's grace."

Zoe put both hands in the air. "Well, hurry it up, then."

I shook my head. "Sisters." I finished ripping the envelope down the side, and then tipped it, spilling out the flowery note paper. I unfolded it and read out loud.

> *Dear Arcade,*
> *I hope you are having a nice summer. Mine has been quiet since you, your sister, and your nice friend Doug returned to New York City.*

"Aw, she called me nice!" Doug smiled. "Hey! Maybe I could go live with Miss Gertrude."

I continued:

> *Jacey and her mother come to visit me once a week. They bring me the most delicious cinnamon bread . . .*

I stopped. The thought of that cinnamon bread made my mouth water.

"What's wrong, Arcade? Do you miss Jacey?" Zoe reached over and put a hand on my cheek. "Are you blushing?"

I pushed her hand away. "Hey! You should talk—Michael Tolley!" I read on.

> *My grandsons have not returned since the night you finished renovating the windmill course. I think I know what happened to them, and I must warn you ... Do not try to bring them back. I know you have the power to do so, but it is not advised at this time. Trust the tester.*
> *Sincerely, Miss Gertrude*

"Bring them back? Why does she think I have the power to bring them back?"

Zoe pulled the letter from my hand. "It doesn't matter, because she said not to do it. So, don't."

I pulled the token out from under my shirt. "Maybe I really am controlling this! Think about it! I said *flamingo,* and now we have Flames."

"Destroying my bathroom." Doug laughed.

"And before we went to the refinery, I said something to the token. Oh, what did I say?" I closed my eyes tight and tried to relive the scene. "Where did you come from?"

"I'm originally from New Jersey," Doug said.

I opened my eyes. "No, not you, Doug. I asked the *token* to show me where *it* came from. And then it took us to the refinery! Maybe I do have the power to bring the Badgers back!"

Zoe got up from the couch, covering her face with her hands. "Lord, no. This boy cannot control this thing!"

"And when we left the refinery, you asked for food, remember?" Doug threw both hands up in the air. "And we ended up in a fish market!" Doug pointed to my token. "Man, we should go somewhere now! Tell it to take us somewhere, Arcade!"

"No, we SHOULD NOT go somewhere now!" Zoe stomped a foot. "Arcade doesn't know what he's doing! He has no idea what the power of pure gold can do."

I held up my Gold Rush book. "Maybe we can find out here." As soon as I said that, it was like the Triple T Token turned into a tiny firework on my chest. It jumped and blew out a few sparks toward Doug and Zoe. They jumped back.

"Don't do it, Arcade! DON'T DO IT!" And as soon as *she* said that, showers of gold flakes fell from the ceiling.

"Well, it looks like we're going somewhere. Glitter never lies." I held out my hands and caught several gold flakes.

Doug ran in the kitchen and brought out a few pie tins. "Here! Catch it, just in case it's real!"

"This isn't real gold, Doug." Zoe said. "It's glitter."

I looked a little closer at the bits in my hand, pressing and moving them around with my finger. It had a different texture than glitter. "Uh, Zoe. I think Doug might be on to something." Loopy came bounding down the stairs. "Hey, Loop! You wanna go on a gold adventure?" Loopy barked and tried to lick some of the gold flakes off my shoe.

"No way, Arcade."

I looked at my sister with a smile. "Aw, c'mon. We wouldn't want to disappoint Loopy." I picked him up with one hand and rested the hot token in my other. "Show us the power of pure gold!" I shouted. A large fountain of sparks flew out of the center of the token, and gold elevator doors appeared in the middle of the living room. "Grab the book!" I yelled to Doug.

I held Loopy tight and pulled the token from the chain. It came loose, and a golden coin slot shaped like a miner's pan appeared in front of the doors. I threw the token in, and they opened.

CHAPTER 15

Preteen 49ers

"These elevators are getting fancier," Zoe said as the doors closed behind us. She walked around, smoothing her hand along all four walls. "If I didn't think it was impossible, I'd say these walls are made of pure gold."

"Why would it be impossible? Don't you see? I asked the token to show us the power of pure gold, and here we are."

Zoe gave me an intense stare. "Arcade, *why* are you doing this? What if this adventure doesn't turn out the way you want?"

"Zoe, remember what you said to me in the elevator at the refinery? What if I never opened another library book? Maybe *that's* the test. To see if I'm adventurous and open to new things."

"NO! It's to test your *mettle*, remember? You heard the lady! Where is that brain of yours?"

I didn't have time to answer, because the doors opened and Loopy ran out.

"Loopy! Get back here!"

We chase Loopy down a sloshy, mud path, getting sloppier each moment from cold, pouring rain. After our blazing summer in New York City, the cold is a welcome feeling . . . until I start to shiver as water drips down my back.

"Loopy!"

Loopy stops on the banks of a river, where several rugged-looking young men in dirty clothes and tattered hats are squatting, holding something out in the water.

"They're gold panning!" Doug says. "Good thing I brought pans!"

Zoe puts an arm out to stop us. "I don't think we should go down there."

I push through. "Too late. Loopy's already there."

He's sitting between a couple of the guys, and one of them is petting him while Loopy licks mud off his fingers. "You're a sight for sore eyes, pup. Where'd you come from?" The young man stands, stretches, and turns around. He almost falls into the river when he sees us. "Hey, you kids! What are you doin' down here? This your dog?"

That gets the attention of all the men, who also stand and stare.

"I'm thinking we look out of place," I say quietly through clenched teeth.

"Ya think?" Zoe replies.

The tallest man, who also looks to be the oldest, walks a few steps our way. "You lookin' for somethin', young people? Come down here."

"I don't wanna go." Doug backs up a step. I reach for his sleeve and pull him along with us anyway.

I clear my throat. "Hello, sir. My name is uh, Arcade—"

The man scrunches up his face. "Arcade? Like the architecture? All them arches?"

I grin. "Well, yeah, that's one of the meanings of the word, but I like to think it's more like a gaming arcade."

The guy raises an eyebrow. "Gaming? You mean like gamblin'?"

Zoe cuts in. "NO. Not like that at all. Like a . . . uh . . . penny arcade."

The guy gives me a blank stare. "Don't have a clue about no penny arcade." He puts his hand on my shoulder and grips hard. He pushes me down to the edge of the river. "So, what do you want, Mr. Arches?" He laughs, and the rest of the gang joins him. "You wanna join the crew? We're about to score big on this claim. Got ourselves a valuable piece of the river to mine."

I look around at the ripped canvas tents, and the skinny men in holey shoes and shirts. By the smell of them, I wonder if they ran out of money for soap months ago.

"Thanks for the offer, sir, but we just came for our dog." Zoe backs away and waves me back.

One of the other guys comes up behind Doug and points to the pie pans. "Looks like you came to do some minin'." Then he squints and looks closer. "Hey, what's all this? Where you been dunking your pans, partner?"

He fingers the gold glitter in the pan. Pushes it around a few seconds.

Please don't let that be real gold.

The man pulls the pan from Doug's hand and gives it to the old guy. "Check this out, boss!"

The old guy fishes around in the pan and holds his gold-covered finger up close to Doug's face. "Where'd you get this, kid?"

"Uh, Arcade's living room. Just came from there. This stuff was falling from the ceiling."

The younger man pushes Doug in the chest and he falls into the mud, dropping the other pan. Loopy runs over and sits in Doug's lap.

"Ain't never heard of no gold fallin' from no ceilin'. You know what I think? I think maybe we got some claim jumpers here, boss!" The man picks the pan up out of the mud and hands it to the old miner.

He stares into the pan. "You kids been pannin' in my part of the river?"

I shake my head, hard. "No, sir. We would never do that. We were just trying to find my dog."

The leathery prospector stares at my face, but then his eyes drop to my neck. "What's that chain you got there?"

Zoe steps in between us. "I'm sorry we disturbed your gold mining. We'll be taking our dog and going now."

The miner brushes her aside. "What are you doin' down

here, little lady? Shouldn't you be in the city with the other women mendin' socks or somethin'?"

Oh, boy.

Zoe crosses her arms and sticks out her chin. "I BEG YOUR PARDON? Mending socks? And who are YOU to be telling ME what I should be doing?"

"Sassy," one of the guys says, and a bunch of them laugh.

The man reaches out and grabs my chain. And right at that moment, the token appears back on it, shining all pure-gold like.

Bad timing! Bad timing!

The guy rests my token in his hand. "Triple T, huh? What *is* this?" He holds it to his mouth and bites the token. I hear a sizzle on his tongue.

"Hey! That's hot gold!" At the sound of his cry, all the miners crowd around me.

"Where'd you get that, kid? That's a huge chunk for just one person. You wanna share?" All of a sudden, hands are reaching out, all trying to pull Triple T off the chain.

"Yeah, kids don't need gold. And we're starvin' out here! You're on our claim, so I'm thinkin' that's ours!"

"Run, Arcade!" Zoe reaches for my hand, tugs hard, and pulls me from the huddle. Loopy is at my feet. I grab him up, duck through a hole in the group, and start to run and slip through the mud.

Doug scrambles up the bank and calls to me from the top. "We need some doors, Arcade! Summon the doors!"

Summon the doors?

"I've never done that before!" I shout back. "They're supposed to just . . . show up!"

By now, the prospectors are breathing down my neck, so I gotta try something.

I trap the sizzling token between my palms. It pulses light and heat. "Get us back home!" I yell. Golden doors appear at the top of the bank, and the coin slot pushes out from the middle.

"Thank goodness!" Zoe yells. "Throw it in, Arcade!"

I pull the Triple T Token off the chain and, just as I reach the top of the muddy bank, I flip it into the slot. A huge golden mining trough appears on the top of the elevator doors. I motion with my hands for the doors to open. They do, and Zoe, Doug, Loopy, and I run in. We turn just in time to see the prospectors about to enter the elevator with us. But right before they do, the trough tilts down, sending a stream of golden glitter slush all over them.

"Eureka!" I yell.

The doors close.

We landed back in my living room. Muddy, but just us. No prospectors in sight.

Zoe grabs me by the collar. "EUREKA? We barely avoid disaster with greedy prospectors and you yell, 'EUREKA'?"

I picked a clump of dried mud off my elbow and grinned. "Eureka is the state motto of California. It means

'I found it!' I read it right here in my library book . . . uh-oh . . ." I looked over at Doug, who had his fist up to his mouth. "What happened to the book, Doug?"

"What happened to the book?"

"That's what I said, Doug."

"You told me to grab the book on the way out."

"Yeaaaah."

"So I did."

"And?"

"You didn't tell me to grab it on the way back. So I guess it's like the opposite of Eureka, you know? Because I didn't find it, I lost—"

"Doug! Do you know how much I *hate* to lose library books? How am I supposed to explain this to Ms. Weckles? Borrowing a book is a privilege that I take very seriously!"

Doug slumped down on the floor. "Sorry, Arcade. I got kinda scared when that guy pushed me in the mud."

Zoe stood up and rubbed mud off her arms. "Doug, you shouldn't be apologizing. This is all Arcade's fault."

"WHAT? How is this *my* fault?"

"HOW is it your fault? How about THIS? 'We can't disappoint Loopy. Show us the power of pure gold,'" she said in an exaggerated mocking tone. "Don't you remember your own words, Arcade? You couldn't just ignore it, could you?"

"I've never been able to ignore it, Zoe. The thing heats up, glitter falls, and we go somewhere. You know that."

"But now you're *commanding* it! You're going where YOU want to go. And this time you lost a book. And you almost lost your token. Who knows what else you could have lost! And what did you learn, exactly? Did you learn what the power of pure gold is? I don't think so! Because it looks to me like gold CORRUPTS people. You saw the greed in those prospectors' eyes. It wasn't good, Arcade. And guess what? I think that was the same look you had on your face right before you decided to take us through those doors."

Ouch.

"So . . . just sayin' . . . if that old woman on top of the Empire State Building was right, and the token really is testing you—I'd say you failed this time."

The front door opened, and in walked Mom and Dad. Their smiles turned to confused frowns when they got a look at us.

"Mud? Really? In the *living room*?" Mom ran upstairs and came down dragging a steam cleaner and holding a stack of towels. "I expect this to be cleaned up immediately."

Dad just stood with his hand on his hip. "It's dry as the Sahara Desert outside. Where in the world did you get muddy?" Then he tipped his head, looked into my eyes, and grinned. "I'm glad school starts tomorrow. Seems like you all need something better to do with your time."

Zoe thumped on my bedroom door to wake Doug and me up for the first day of school. It's a weird tradition that she insists on never breaking. But this time, I was ready for her! I flung the door open and jumped in her face. "HA! You thought I'd still be sleeping, didn't you? Well, I'm changing my ways, sister!"

Zoe gave me a once over and then stared at me, stone-faced. "Sleep in your clothes again?"

"Maybe. But at least my clothes are stylish."

She rolled her eyes. "Whatever. I'm off to the subway. I'm going early today so I can find all my classes. Michael said he'd help."

"Oh, so that's why you brushed your hair," I said with a little wiggle of my head.

Zoe reached out and grabbed my token. "Remember our agreement. You don't go anywhere with this thing without me. If it heats up, do whatever you need to do. Douse it. Jump into the Hudson River, the Central Park reservoir, or the nearest aquarium. You got it?"

I leaned on the door and smirked. "Yeah, I got it."

She turned to leave. I almost closed the door, but then she came back and pushed through. "Arcade?"

"Yeah?"

"Have a good first day of middle school." She reached out, gave me a hug, smiled, and disappeared down the stairs.

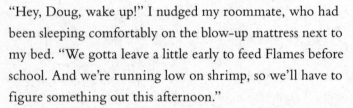

"Hey, Doug, wake up!" I nudged my roommate, who had been sleeping comfortably on the blow-up mattress next to my bed. "We gotta leave a little early to feed Flames before school. And we're running low on shrimp, so we'll have to figure something out this afternoon."

"Ugh. What day is it?" Doug sat up and scratched his head.

"It's the first day of middle school! You know, every kid's nightmare."

Doug fell back. "Wiley's gonna punch my lights out when he sees me."

"I doubt it. He probably won't even recognize you. You're like a mile tall now." I smacked the bottom of Doug's foot that hung out over the mattress.

Doug cracked his neck. "I guess I do look a little different now."

"What does this Wiley Overton look like, anyway? Do you think *you'll* recognize *him*?"

Doug thought a minute. "Oh yeah, I'll recognize him. I've seen him around the city a few times since third grade.

Hasn't changed a bit, except he's gotten huger. I've always thought he looked like a big potato."

Adrenaline surged through my veins. "What kind of potato, exactly?"

"Well, definitely not a sweet potato."

Loopy met me at the bottom of the stairs for my morning lick of encouragement. "Loop, I wish you could come." I thought for a second about stuffing him in my backpack to see if I could pass him off as my seventh-grade therapy dog. I hugged him tight instead. "I'll see you this afternoon." Then I placed him behind the dog gate in the kitchen.

My dad, who works into the early mornings because of his job, had left me a note on the dining room table. I picked it up and read it out loud to Doug.

Dear Arcade,
Middle School! What a challenge. But you can handle it! Remember your #GOALZ. And also remember this:
'My son, never let loyalty and kindness leave you! Tie them around your neck as a reminder. Write them deep within your heart. Then you will find favor with both God and people, and you will earn a good reputation.' Proverbs 3:3–4 NLT.

Love, Dad

"I like that part about tying them around your neck," Doug said. "Sounds like your token."

"Yeah, I guess it does. Hey, Doug, you got a note too." I held the three-by-five card out to him.

"Really? That's cool!" He took it from me and read it.

Dear Doug,
We love having you with us. This is going to be a great year for you. Don't worry about anything! God's got you!
                                        Mr. Livingston

Doug breathed in deep and carefully folded the card. He put it in his back pocket. "I'm keepin' this." Then he looked up at me. "What's for breakfast?"

MS 230 is four blocks north and two blocks east from my house. It sits right across from Central Park. Sweet.

"Dude, I miss your flamingo backpack." Doug jogged along next to me on the way to school. Our bodies didn't feel like walking on this nerve-filled morning.

"Me too." I reached up to tighten the straps on my second favorite backpack, the one with multiple colors running through a black background. "But we got a real flamingo now, remember?"

"How can I forget? Arcade, what are we gonna do with that bird? Pretty soon realtors are gonna wanna bring some buyers over to my place, and I can't have it smelling like shrimp. Or . . . worse."

I scratched my head. "I don't know. Maybe I can ask the token to take us back to Beijing." The token shot a hot blast through my chest. I grabbed it. "But not right now!"

"Hey, Arcade! Doug!" The sound of a puttering electric scooter behind us signaled that the most fun kid in all of New York City had arrived.

Thomas Scranton. I call him Scratchy.

"Scratchy! Dude!" I ran up and gave him a high-five. "How was your summer?"

Scratchy wiped sweat from his freckly, fair-skinned neck. "Hot! Man, you wouldn't believe how many tubes of sunscreen I went through. And I got scorched anyway!" Scratchy scratched his shoulder. "I'm shedding skin like a snake." Behind Scratchy was another kid I didn't know riding in an electric wheelchair. "Guys, this is Carlos James C.J. Mendoza. He's a RADICAL daredevil. Just moved onto my street last week."

I reached out a fist. "Hey, dude. Nice to meet ya. Do I have to call you all those names?"

"Nah. You can pick. I answer to all of them."

"Cool! I like options. Today I'll call you Carlos."

"Works for me."

"How'd you score that sweet ride?" Doug asked, pointing to the wheelchair. I cringed a little at his bold question and waited nervously to see how Carlos would respond.

"Thanks for asking. Car accident. A drunk driver plowed through a red light and t-boned our car. We were on our way to celebrate my ninth birthday at the trampoline park that day."

"Ah, man, I'm sorry." I didn't know what else to say.

"Thanks. It's been a rough couple of years, but I'm making it through."

"Carlos here is a bomb gymnast," Scratchy said.

"I can still walk on my hands at least." Carlos smiled and swiped his hand over his perfectly smooth, dark-brown hair. "This city is a little tough to get around, though. It's a good thing I can pop wheelies in this thing. We moved to the Upper West Side because the paths in the park are easier for me to navigate than the city streets."

"Those are some nice wheels," I said. "How do you get down the stairs to the subway?"

Carlos smiled and pulled out a map. "This map shows all the subway stations that are wheelchair accessible."

"Not all of them are?" I had never noticed before.

"I wish." Carlos laughed.

"Sounds like he needs to have a portable elevator show up whenever he needs it. *That* would be sweet." Doug elbowed me so hard I almost flew into the street. At the same time, my token steamed and sent out two bolts of heat, one to my head, the other to my feet.

"Are you all ready to do this MS 230 thing?" Scratchy asked.

"I am." Carlos pulled another paper out of his backpack. "Do any of you have homeroom with Dooley?"

"YES!" We all yelled.

"Is that good?"

I laughed. "Yeah, Dooley's cool. But you should try to sit in the back row. Easier on the ears."

Carlos shrugged and popped a wheelie. "I just hope they'll have a desk I can use with this thing."

"Aw, man, I never thought about that before."

"I never thought about it either, until two years ago. But hey, I go with the flow now. At least I never have to worry about having a chair to sit in, right?"

"Carlos, you're so RAD. I'm glad you're in our class." Scratchy revved his scooter. "Let's go do this middle school thing!"

"Yeah! Let's do this middle school thing!" Doug jumped up and down and pounded his chest.

"Yeah! This is gonna be good!" I reached for the token and jogged next to Carlos as he wheeled along toward the entrance to MS 230.

At least I hope so.

"WELCOME TO SEVENTH GRADE HOMEROOM!" Mr. Dooley boomed. We all flew back in our seats. "Okay, now that you're awake . . ." Mr. Dooley went to the whiteboard and scrawled his name. Then he turned and gave us a goofy grin. "You kids from PS 23 didn't think you'd get rid of me that easily, did you?"

I scanned the room. Some kids were strangers that had come from other schools. Others were not. Bailey Martin and Amber Lin, two girls who had been on my Triple T

Team for the sixth-grade career expo, sat together on the opposite side of the room. And, unfortunately, the Tolley brothers sat in the middle of the room like they did in sixth grade, smirking and grunting. Doug, Scratchy, and I had taken the back row, not only to save our ears, but also to sit with our new friend Carlos who had found one desk wheelchair accessible in the corner.

Right as the tardy bell rang, the door to the classroom creaked open. A huge kid, dressed in faded jeans and an oversized, rumpled brown T-shirt, walked in.

Some of the kids started to whisper to each other. The big kid scanned the room for an empty seat. The only one was in the front row, closest to the door.

"That's him." Doug leaned over to whisper to me. "That's Wiley."

Mr. Dooley finished writing on the board.

MR. DOOLEY–HOMEROOM–MATH AND SCIENCE.

"AS I SAID BEFORE, WELCOME TO SEVENTH GRADE HOMEROOM." Mr. Dooley hopped up to sit on his desk. "This year, I'll only be testing you in the areas of math and science. If you're wondering why I followed you to this school, I'll just say this . . ."

We all leaned forward. I expected him to say that he couldn't live without us, or something flattering like that.

". . . there was an opening, and I took it."

"There was an opening and you took it?"

"Yes, Mr. Baker. You heard me correctly."

Doug turned to me. "There was an opening and he took it."

Mr. Dooley continued. "Now, I know that some of you struggle with math. Here's why I think that is. Most of you don't like to have just one answer to a question. But to me, math is comforting, because there is just one answer! Two plus two is four. Four plus four is eight." He grinned. "See? Isn't that relaxing?" He laced his fingers together and placed them behind his head. "Doesn't that make you want to sink into a plush beanbag chair and take a nap?"

No one responded. Mr. Dooley began to walk around the room. "Now, science, that's a totally different story. Science is all about discovery! As we discover new things about our world, science changes. For example, is Pluto a planet or not? It was. Then it wasn't. Fascinating, yet not so comfortable."

"I never liked that Pluto got demoted," I whispered to Scratchy.

"I thought Pluto was a dog," one of the Tolleys blurted out. There was a little bit of nervous laughter from a few other students.

I raised my hand.

"Yes, Mr. Livingston?"

"Ummm . . . but Pluto never changed. We just changed the way we looked at it, right?"

Mr. Dooley rubbed his chin. "Correct."

"So doesn't that make science *just* like math? I mean, Pluto is Pluto. Two plus two is four. Relax in the beanbag."

Now all the kids laughed.

Hey! I'm serious!

In the past, when I've asked questions like that, I'd been given detention because the teacher thought I was being disrespectful. So when Mr. Dooley approached and tapped my desk with his pencil, I expected the worst.

"Keep on asking questions, Mr. Livingston. Because without questions, there is no learning." Then he walked back to the front of the class. "Open your math books and get your ears ready to listen. We'll be having a test next Friday, so I hope your brains haven't become mush over the summer." Mr. Dooley inserted a little key in his top right desk drawer and pulled out a stack of stiff forms. "These are what we in middle school call computer scan forms. Get used to the look of them. You'll enter your test answers here. MANY A STUDENT HAS FAILED A TEST because they lost concentration, skipped a row, and FILLED IN THE WRONG BUBBLE. Here's a tip for surviving middle school. ALWAYS PAY ATTENTION WHEN YOU ARE BEING TESTED."

A gasp sounded from the other side of the room. It was Bailey Martin. She's super smart, and a straight-A student, but she's more than a bit anxious. She turned pale at the sight of the computer scan sheets.

Carlos leaned over to me. "What is that snapping sound?"

"It's probably Bailey. She's cracking her knuckles under the desk. She does that."

Carlos nodded. "Oh. I thought it was coming from over there."

I looked in the other direction. Wiley Overton was staring right at me! And he was cracking his knuckles too.

CHAPTER 17

Coop

I kept a secret eye on Wiley all through the morning during class, and then searched for him in the lunch room. Thankfully he didn't sit at our table with us. "Hey, Doug. I don't know why but I feel like I've seen Wiley somewhere before."

Doug spoke through a mouth full of hamburger. "You think you've seen Wiley somewhere before?"

"Yeah. And he was staring at me all morning, like he knows me or something." Our table started filling up, so we dropped our conversation down to a whisper. I pulled out my phone. "I have an idea. Let's stand up, face his direction, and pretend to take a selfie. Instead, I'll take a picture of Wiley. Then I'll text it to Zoe. Maybe she'll recognize him too."

"Great idea, bro." Doug washed down his last bite of burger with a huge chug of milk and then came and stood next to me. "You and me buddy! First day of school selfie!" He said it loud enough for the whole cafeteria to hear.

I stood there, my fingers trembling a little, as I zoomed

in on Wiley. I held the camera up. *Yep, that's a good shot. Oh, wait, he's getting larger . . .*

Someone pulled my phone out of my hands.

"You trying to break your phone, Livingston?"

Caught!

"Um, no. I'm just trying to take a picture. As you can see, the screen is already cracked. Accident in the subway a couple of weeks ago. Lost my backpack too."

"Ooooh. Tragic." Wiley narrowed his eyes at me and then turned his attention toward Doug. "You remember me, Baker?"

Doug nodded. "Yeah. How you doin', Wiley?"

"I'm doin' great. Just great. You havin' eye trouble lately?"

"Eye trouble?" Doug's hand flew up to his right eye.

"Yeah. You and four-eyes here seem to be having trouble seeing this phone screen. You see, to take a selfie, you gotta flip the camera by clicking this tiny square. Ha! You almost got a picture of me by accident. And even as handsome as I am, I'm sure that's not what you were trying to do."

"That would DEFINITELY break the phone." Wiley stepped aside. Standing behind him was a short, light-skinned girl with brown, shoulder-length curls and a couple of really deep dimples that caved in her cheeks while she smirked. She elbowed Wiley out of the way and set her lunch tray down next to the chair where Doug was standing.

"Coop?!?" Doug gasped. "I thought you moved to Texas."

The girl snatched the phone out of Wiley's hands and gave it back to me. "I did. But we missed the city, so we moved back."

"Hey, girlie." Wiley tried to push back in. "We were talking here."

Coop put her hand up in Wiley's face. "Whiny, you just need to go way. No one at this table wants to hear *anything* from you."

Wiley glared at the brave girl for a minute, but she just glared back.

She stuck out her chin. "What? Are you gonna punch me? Go right ahead. I dare ya. Get yourself expelled for the millionth time." She glared some more.

So did Wiley. Finally, he turned and went back to the table where Casey and Kevin Tolley were eating. Wiley said something to the guys, and they all looked over at us and laughed.

Coop shook her head. "Ignore them. They're bad news. Doug, who's your friend?"

"I'm Arcade."

"I'm Reagan Cooper. Nice to meet you. Doug and I have been friends since kindergarten. I moved away in the 4th grade. But I'm back now. With a drawl, y'all!" Her eyes twinkled. "How's your grandma, Doug?" Reagan turned to me. "Doug's gram is the sweetest person I've ever met." Reagan reached into her backpack and pulled out her phone. "I know! Let's take a selfie, Doug."

"Yeah. Let's take a selfie!" Doug got up and stood next to Reagan. She held her phone up, smiled, clicked the picture, and then they both sat down.

She whispered to me. "I just got that picture of Wiley for you."

"How'd you know?"

She grinned. "I'm sneaky. It's a gift. I think it may come in handy in middle school. What do you think?" She turned her phone around for me to see it. And there, right in the middle of the screen, was Wiley Overton's mug, enlarged to fit the whole screen, clear as day.

After lunch, I texted the picture to Zoe.

This guy look familiar???

I got a text back immediately.

It's him! The sack of potatoes!

I almost dropped my phone. *Just as I thought.* I could barely keep my hands still enough to text back.

He's at my school.

All she texted back was . . .

Uh-oh.

CHAPTER 18

Bye, Bye, Doug

That night, Doug and I sat around studying chapter one in our math books.

"I don't know, Arcade, this stuff looks hard. And now I'm supposed to worry about filling in the right bubbles? Maybe we should ditch the studying and go feed Flames."

I sat staring at the computer scan sheet, replaying Mr. Dooley's words over and over in my head:

"ALWAYS PAY ATTENTION WHEN YOU ARE BEING TESTED."

The Triple T Token heated up a little, and I pulled my shirt away from my chest to check it out.

"What?"

"I said, maybe we should ditch this and go feed Flames."

I looked up at Doug. "Huh? Oh, I wasn't talking to you. I was talking to this . . . this . . . token. Whenever it sparks, it puts me on edge."

"Tell me about it! We've been on a ton of edges! Why do edges always lead to huge drop offs?"

"They don't. You just notice those more."

"Nah. ALL edges are dangerous."

Doug's phone rang. He took a deep breath. "An unrecognized number. Here we go . . ." He put it on speaker. "Hello?"

"Hello, is this Doug?"

"Doug?"

"Yes, Doug. Doug Baker."

"I'm Doug Baker."

The woman on the other end of the phone sighed. "Oh, good. Hi, Doug. My name is Charlotte Schmidt. We talked a couple of weeks ago."

Silence.

"I'm your social worker. I'd like to come see you tomorrow."

Doug's fingers started to tremble, and he dropped his phone on his blow-up mattress. "Tomorrow? That's not necessary. I'm not in any hurry."

"But I have great news! Your Aunt Tianna is excited for you to come and live with her."

Doug shot up on his feet. "Aunt Tianna?"

"Mmmm-hmmm. Your mom's sister."

Doug made a face like he just chewed a lemon. Then he looked at me and mouthed the words SHE'S AWFUL.

"Aw, no. I'll pass. Who else you got?"

There was a moment of silence on the other side of the phone. "Uh, well, I appreciate your input, Doug, but this is actually your only option. Your aunt already has your room set up and has enrolled you in a private school in Miami Beach."

"Miami Beach? Like, in Florida?"

"Well, yes, that's where your aunt lives. I know it will be an adjustment, but the weather is beautiful in Florida."

Doug reached over and clicked his phone off.

"DOUG! Did you just hang up on her?"

"Yeah. Should I block her?" He scrolled to his phone settings, but I grabbed his wrist before he could finish.

The phone rang again. I put my hand on Doug's shoulder. "Answer it."

"Awww, man!" He put it on speaker again.

"Doug? I'm sorry, for some reason we got cut off."

"Hello, Ms. Schmidt. Yeah, sorry. That was my fault."

"That's okay. So, Doug, I'd like to come and meet with you tomorrow. I know our official meeting wasn't for a couple of weeks yet, but the sooner we get you to your new home the better. School starts down there in a week. Can I come to your house in the afternoon?"

"MY HOUSE?" Doug looked over at me, stuck his hands out like wings, and curled one leg up. "I don't think that's a good idea."

"Oookay. Would another location work better?"

I pointed to my floor. Doug raised his eyebrows.

"We could meet in my friend Arcade's room."

I shook my head and pointed to my bedroom door.

"Uh, no. I mean my friend Arcade's *house*. It's just three doors down from my place."

"Oh, yes. The Livingston's. I have their address right here in my file. That would be fine. Would four o'clock work?"

"Would four o'clock work?" Doug looked like he was going to faint. "I guess."

"Great! I'll give you more details when we meet. This is going to be a great new start for you, Doug. You may want to start packing your things. I'm hopeful we can finalize the paperwork and get you a one-way flight to your new home in Miami by the end of next week."

"Arcade, what am I gonna do? I don't want to move to Florida!" Doug and I plodded all the way down to the greenstone to check on Flames.

My mind raced.

What can I do? I don't want my best friend to move.

I pulled my token out from under my shirt and held it between my hands.

This would be a good time for you to show me your power.

Nothing happened. Not even a spark. In fact, the token felt so cold, it sent shivers through my body, even though it was at least ninety degrees out!

We walked up the steps to the greenstone, and Doug put the key in the lock and sniffed. "I'm gonna miss the smell of shrimp." He opened the door and took a long glance around. "This could be my last week in New York City."

We dragged ourselves up the stairs and opened the door to Flames's "office." The little bird flapped and squawked and splashed when he saw us.

"Hey, buddy! Sorry it took so long. Are you hungry?" I opened the lid of the ice chest we had set up in the bathroom and pulled out a small sandwich bag of shrimp. I reached in and held a piece in my palm. Flames squawked and waddled over. An orange glow surrounded him. Or . . .

"Hey, Arcade! Look at that! He's ORANGE!"

I reached out to pet Flames's feathers. Sure enough, the little guy was gaining his color!

"That's DOPE! Wait till Zoe sees this!"

At the sound of her name, big sis walked in the bathroom. "You guys should really learn to lock a door behind you. Any knucklehead could have come in here."

I laughed. "Yep. You're proof."

Zoe thumped me on the back of the head.

"Zoe, check this out! What color do you think Flames is?"

Zoe crossed her arms and tilted her head. "He's shrimp-colored." She held her arm next to Flames, matching his wings to a bracelet she was wearing. "A perfect match to this pink bracelet."

Flames squawked at Zoe and pecked at the sandwich bag full of shrimp. I pulled out another piece and held it in my palm. Flames devoured it.

"You know, Arcade, he's getting bigger. He's going to need more food each day. I don't think our budget can handle buying much more shrimp."

"And I'm moving to Florida, so he won't be able to stay here much longer," Doug said.

Zoe's head snapped around. "You're moving to FLORIDA?"

"I'm moving to Florida. Unless someone can find me a way out of it."

And for the first time, Zoe asked me a question that was

the exact opposite of any she'd asked before when it came to the Triple T.

"Arcade, can your token do anything?"

I shook my head. "It's as cold as ice."

My whole family took Doug to the airport the next Thursday night. Hardly a word was spoken the entire car ride.

The loudspeaker boomed its final warning:

"Flight 623 to Miami, Florida will be boarding in thirty minutes. Any passengers not yet through the security checkpoint should make their way through now."

Doug and I stood there, stunned. "I can't believe this is happening." Anger and sadness boiled up inside of me.

How am I going to get through this year without Doug?

"Yeah, man, and I really wanted to take that math test tomorrow." Doug chuckled and poked me with his elbow. But then tears started to flow. He covered his face and breathed deeply in and out. I did the same.

"Don't worry, Doug," I said, my voice cracking with emotion. "If there's any way to get you back here, I'll find it."

Doug reached over and shoved something into my hand.

"Here's the key to the greenstone. The realtor lady said she's coming to put some new locks on it in a few days. I'll text you when for sure. Until then, Flames can have the run of the place."

I grabbed the key. "Thanks, Doug. You're the best. I'll

miss y—" But I couldn't finish. It was just too painful to see my best friend go.

"Yeah. I'll miss you too."

"Doug, your security wand awaits." My dad picked Doug's super stuffed backpack up off the floor and handed it to him. Then, he put his hands on both of Doug's shoulders and closed his eyes.

"Lord, watch over our friend Doug. Help him adjust to his new home. Give him great friends who will support him and appreciate his sense of humor. Give him peace and understanding about the big changes ahead. And above all, Lord, give him great food! We trust you with his life. Amen."

I couldn't even look up. Tears fell and splashed on the floor. All of a sudden, airports were my least favorite place in the whole world.

And this one was *super hot*!

"We're gonna go hang out over here at the coffee kiosk," Dad said. "You guys can walk Doug over to security."

Mom stepped forward and gave Doug a big hug. "Keep in touch," she said. She had tears in her eyes as she left with Dad.

I walked over to the security line with my sister and my best friend.

"Bye, Doug," I said, but he didn't repeat me this time.

"I'm not sayin' it," Doug said. "Cause I'm comin' back."

Zoe gave Doug a hug. "If you need anything, call, text, email, whatever."

"I won't need anything. Aunt Tianna has everything. She's got a fancy place full of furniture you can't sit on and towels you can't use."

Then, Zoe's red, puffy eyes grew wide as she put a hand on my shoulder. "Arcade, I *really* wish I didn't have to say this right now, but your token is blinding me."

I tried to look down at the Triple T, but it shined so bright I had to shield my eyes.

Of course! That's why I'm so hot!

I took the pulsing token in my hand. "Show me a home for Doug. Somewhere we can be together!" And as soon as I spoke those words, Doug's backpack began to glow red! Two pipes shot out from the bottom of the backpack and started spewing yellow and orange glitter, surrounding Doug in a colorful cloud.

"Arcade!" Doug shouted out from the orange and yellow mist. "I gotta get through security or I'll miss my flight!"

"Uh-oh." Zoe reached out and gripped my arm. "Where are we off to this time?"

Doug jumped out of the cloud, shaking glitter from his hair. "Security will never let me through with a flaming jet pack!"

I shook my head. "I don't think you're headed for Florida just yet. This little metal tester might show us your new home!"

"It's going to show us my new home?"

"That's what I said. Somewhere we can be together."

"Arcade, what did you say to it?" Zoe moved in close and shoved us over to a corner, next to a monitor showing flight arrivals and departures. The writing blurred and then it also turned to glitter. The monitor enlarged and became elevator doors. Airport travelers scurried by us like none of this was happening.

The golden coin slot popped out, just as Doug's jet pack began to lift him off the ground. He grabbed me and held on tight. "I have a bad feeling about this!"

I reached for my token, pulled it off the chain, and glanced over at Zoe. "We *all* go in, and we *all* return, with *everything* we brought with us. We'll be as careful as anything and we won't talk to a living soul."

Zoe threw up her hands. "Throw it in."

I grinned and deposited the coin in the slot. The doors opened. When we walked in, we were immediately covered in puffy suits. And helmets.

Wait . . . these aren't helmets . . . they're . . .

"Space suits!" Doug yelled. Well, he yelled as much as he could with a voice muffled by his . . .

SPACE SUIT?!?

The doors closed. Doug's jet pack spewed out more glitter. A voice over the speaker began to count down . . .

"10 . . . 9 . . . 8 . . ."

"Arcade, where are we going?!?"

"I have no idea. But you hate heights. So at least we're counting down instead of up, right?" Doug didn't look the least bit relieved.

"7 . . . 6 . . . 5 . . . 4 . . ."

Zoe, who was outfitted in a shrimpy-pink colored SPACE SUIT, jumped in between me and Doug and linked arms. "Oh, we're counting down all right. But we're going up. So you boys better brace yourselves."

"AHHHHHHHH! I don't wanna go! I'm a food dude, not an astronaut!"

"3 . . . 2 . . . 1 . . . we have ignition . . ."

"IGNITION!" we all shouted.

The elevator began to rumble and shake. The noise was deafening! I tried to cover my ears, but my head was in a SPACE SUIT.

"THIS . . . IS . . . DOOOOOOOOOOPE . . . . . ."

Blastoff!

CHAPTER 19

Moon Walk

We're all laying on the floor, looking up. The elevator stops, and now, we're . . . *floating up.*

"Grab something!" Zoe yells.

"What? The ceiling?" I reach up and brace for impact. But then I just float there, weightless, in the middle of the elevator.

"Arcade, where on earth did you take us?" Doug is doing out-of-control barrel rolls in the elevator.

My heart starts to pound. I can't believe what I'm about to say. "Um, I don't think we're *on* earth anymore, bro."

I've studied a little bit about space. And I've watched enough movies to know that when an astronaut floats away into space, he floats away FOREVER.

If these doors open and we really are in space . . .

I glance over at Zoe, who is turning a cartwheel. "Hey, Zoe! You're finally coordinated!"

Zoe glares at me through her fogged-up face shield. "NOT FUNNY, Arcade! I'm not TRYING to do this!"

"Oh. That's too bad, then."

"Get over here and help me!"

As much as I want to let my sister just flip there a while, I float over and steady her. And that's when I notice all three of us are tethered to a hook inside the elevator.

Whew, that's a relief!

The doors open. And we all drop to the floor.

"Oof!" I sit there in a heap and assess the damage to my body. "That didn't hurt as much as I thought it would. Where are we?"

I stand, take a floaty, semi-weightless step toward the doors, and peer out.

"Well, what do you see?" Doug asks, with a slight tremor in his voice.

"We're definitely sitting on some kind of planetary surface. Wanna take a look around?" Doug and Zoe have plastered themselves to the back corners of the elevator.

"Are there edges?" Doug holds on tighter to his tether.

I tap my foot on the ground. "Not that I can see."

"I'm not sure we should go out there, Arcade. If we're in space, we won't be able to breathe."

I take a big breath in and let it out. "I'm thinking we have air in these suits, Zoe. What do you think you're breathing right now?"

"Yes, but how? I mean, what are we connected to? What if it runs out?"

"What are we *connected* to? And you think *I* ask ridiculous questions? Have we EVER known what we're connected to? Look around, Zoe. This elevator doesn't have any cables."

Zoe takes a step forward. "You're right. This whole thing is insane." She turns to Doug. "I guess we should go explore." She grabs Doug by the shoulder and they follow me out.

As we walk, we are kicking up a powder-like dust. The land is barren.

"The sky is so dark." Zoe stares at her shrimp-colored gloves. "How can I see myself when it's so dark?" She reaches down and runs her glove through the dust. Then she stands up and rubs it around in her palms. She glances at me, then falls onto her behind, pointing to the sky. "Arcade! LOOK!"

I turn and look to the sky. I fall too. "Doug, LOOK!"

Doug turns. And, yes, he falls too.

We're staring at a beautiful, blue planet. Well, not the whole thing. About three-quarters of it. There are swirls of white surrounding it, and between the swirls, we can see a continent.

Doug holds a finger up in the air. "Hey, is that Florida? Because if it is, it's gonna take me a lot longer to get there now."

We all stare in awe. I turn to Zoe. "We're on the moon, Zoe!"

"Good observation, Copernicus."

"Why do you think the token brought us *here*? I asked it to take us somewhere we could be together."

"Oh, we're together, all right. And that promise you made about not talking to another living soul is not going to be hard to keep, either."

"Arcade, I think I see New York too! I can see Florida and New York at the SAME TIME." Doug is in his own little world. His finger can't stop circling the blue planet in the sky.

"I asked the token to show us Doug's new home."

"Yep." Zoe gestures toward the earth. "There it is. Maybe you should be just a teeny bit more specific next time."

"But his new home *can't* be Florida. It just can't."

Doug stands and starts picking things up from the ground, examining them. Zoe scoots a little closer to me. "Arcade, do you remember when Dad told us we were going to move to New York City?"

A knot forms in my stomach. "Yeah. I hated that day. Derek and I ran out to the woods and tried to come up with a plan for me to stay."

"Did it work?"

"Well, duh, no. Because, well . . . here we are." I pointed to earth. "I mean, there we are."

"And do you totally hate living in New York City?"

I shrug. "No. I mean, I miss Derek, and some things about Virginia, but it's not so bad. Kinda fun sometimes, actually."

"Sounds like Florida might be better for Doug, don't you think? He'll have family there who can take care of him. That's better than living by himself with a squawking flamingo."

It feels like someone reaches in and squeezes that knot in my stomach. "But he's my *best friend*, Zoe. He likes me no matter what. It's not fair that I have to lose him right when we're starting middle school."

Zoe gives me a shove.

"What's *that* for?"

"I can't believe what I'm hearing! It's not fair to *you?* What about Doug? It doesn't sound like you're thinking about *him* at all. Wow. I never knew you were this self-absorbed."

"SELF-ABSORBED? Says the girl who can't be away from a mirror for more than five minutes."

Zoe gets up and brushes dust off herself. "Fine. Don't listen to me." She goes over and begins helping Doug with his collection.

I stare up at the earth. And for some reason, Mr. Dooley's words pop into my brain.

ALWAYS PAY ATTENTION WHEN YOU ARE BEING TESTED!

Is this a test? If so, I'm not doing so well.

As soon as that thought hits me, something else almost does. It shoots in from outer space, looking like a small meteorite. "Watch out, Zoe!" I push her out of the way, just as the burning object lands at my feet.

"It's the token," I whisper in shock and disbelief.

Zoe and I stand there, staring at the smoldering piece of gold. "Guess it's time to go," she says. There's not an ounce of excitement in her voice. She begins to glide-walk back to the elevator.

Doug approaches me with a smile. "I got what I need." He leaps over to the elevator.

I pick up the token, and it immediately burns a hole in my space glove. I glide-run as fast as I can back to the elevator, where the golden coin slot is waiting. Zoe is looking down at the ground, her arms crossed. I throw the token in.

CHAPTER 20

Burning Through the Atmosphere

ere, I got you a moon rock!" Doug holds out a gray lump and drops it in my hand. "And I got me one too." He winks. "It'll be our little secret."

Okay, this is cool.

"And I got one more." He holds it out for me to look at.

"Who's that one for?"

"It's for Gram. Can you give it to her for me? I'm *really* going to miss her."

Of course, you will. Hey, wait a minute . . .

"How can they take you away from your grandma? She needs to see you on a regular basis. It will be good for her health. And you need to see her too. That would be the best thing for both of you."

Doug rolls his rock around in his palm. "Well, sure, but how are we going to convince—"

I put my hand out. "I don't know. But we'll figure it out. I'll talk to my parents. They'll have some ideas. Maybe they can talk to your social worker. Or maybe . . . hey! I got it! I can't believe I didn't think of this before."

"Think of what before?" Zoe asks.

"We can adopt Doug. He can live with us! And then he can see his grandma whenever he wants."

"Adopt Doug?" Zoe asks with her eyebrows raised. "Good luck convincing Mom and Dad."

"Why not? They love Doug. And remember what Dad said about me finding someone in the city who's been stricken by misfortune? Well, here he is!" I put my arm around Doug.

"Here he is?" Doug points to himself.

"Yeah. Here you are."

We burn through the atmosphere with something we haven't had since we left for the moon. Hope.

"The floor is HOT!" Doug jumps up and down. Flames shoot up from all four corners of the elevator. Sweat rivers rush down our foreheads. "I don't think this elevator has a heat shield! WE'RE TOAST!"

A smoke alarm sounds from some unknown location. It beeps and blares, sending shockwaves from my eardrums to my temples. I try to cover my ears, but I can't reach them because they're inside the stupid space suit.

"What happens next?" Zoe asks. "Splash down?"

"Let's hope not," I say. "Doug has a flight to catch."

"Flight 623, now boarding."

Doug and I stood there, staring at each other. "Bro, you better go through security." Then I pulled him in by the shoulders and whispered, "We'll get you back here, soon. Just have hope." I gave him a playful shove toward the security line. I watched as he ran through the queue, toward the security agent near the arch.

She said something to Doug, he shook his head, she gestured him through . . . and he set off the alarm.

As another agent waved him back, I ran over to the side of the security line. "Doug! The rock!"

Doug reached into his pocket and pulled out the little space souvenir. "I'm sorry, sir. I forgot I have this moon rock." He walked over and put it in a bin on the conveyor. "Could be radioactive. After all, it just burned through the atmosphere."

"A moon rock, huh?" The man went over and took a look. "That's nice. My boy collects rocks too. He also has a great imagination. *Just* burned through the atmosphere," the man said chuckling and shaking his head. "Okay, let's try this again." The man escorted Doug back through the security arch. This time there were no alarms. Doug ran over to the conveyor and retrieved his backpack and his space rock. He held it up. "See you soon, bro!"

Yeah, Doug. Maybe soon you'll be my real brother.

CHAPTER 21

#FAILZ

School the next day was the worst. I was late, because it took longer to feed Flames without Doug. And the "Homeroom Greeter," Wiley Overton, in the first chair next to the door, was not a welcoming sight.

"Where's your pal Doug?" Wiley asked, rubbing his fist with his hand.

I pulled my old backpack off my shoulders. "He moved."

Wiley laughed. "Still scared of me, huh?"

"NO. He's NOT scared of you." I breathed in deep and blew it out.

My face felt like it was on fire. I reached for the token. It was cool. I walked to my row in the back, where my friends Scratchy and Carlos sat, trying to put a broken pen back together.

"One time, I was messing with a spring from one of these things and it dug into my finger!" Scratchy pretended to whimper. "When I showed it to the teacher, she almost fainted!" Carlos and Scratchy laughed. They stopped when they saw me.

"Hey, Arcade," Scratchy said. "I'm real sorry about Doug moving."

"Yeah." Carlos smoothed his hair. "That's a terrible thing. He's a really nice guy."

"Wah, wah, wah, wah! One less goofball in the neighborhood," one of the Tolleys chimed in from the middle of the room. Today they were wearing matching wrinkled blue polo shirts.

"Hey, Tolleys, can one of you smile for me? It will make me feel better." Sure enough, the one with the chipped tooth smiled. Unfortunately, I still couldn't remember which one had the chipped tooth. I gave him a little wave. "Thanks. It means a lot."

"Don't mention it. It's the least I could do after you helped me with my tree house project last year."

Casey! Write it DOWN, Arcade. Casey has the chipped tooth!

"OKAY, PEOPLE. TODAY IS YOUR FIRST TEST OF MIDDLE SCHOOL. I HOPE YOU ARE READY!"

Mr. Dooley was extra loud this morning. He walked over to his desk, inserted a little key in the top right drawer, and pulled out some papers, which he began to pass out. "Bailey, can you please grab a stack of computer scan pages from the back table and make sure every student gets one? DID YOU ALL BRING YOUR NUMBER 2 PENCILS?"

I raised my hand.

"YES, MR. LIVINGSTON? ARE YOU MISSING SOMETHING?"

Besides my best friend?

"Um, yes . . . sir. I . . . uh . . . forgot my pencil."

And I sort of forgot that we were having a test too.

"WELL, YOU ARE IN LUCK, BECAUSE I ALWAYS HAVE PENCILS AVAILABLE FOR THOSE WHO ARE ILL-PREPARED." Mr. Dooley pointed to a jar in the corner by the sink that held a few pencils. They each had a huge plastic sunflower taped to the end. I walked over and grabbed one, sniffed it, and everyone laughed.

"SORRY I HAD TO MAKE THEM SO OBTRUSIVE. IT'S THE ONLY WAY TO BE SURE NO ONE WALKS OUT WITH MY PENCILS!"

By the time I reached my desk, Bailey had made it to the back row with the computer scan sheets. She gave me a sad look. "I'm sorry about Doug. He drove me crazy when we were on the career expo team together, but other times he made me laugh really hard, which eased my anxiety." She placed her last scan sheet on my desk. "Good luck with the test." Then she walked back to her desk, cracking her knuckles.

"YOU HAVE FORTY-FIVE MINUTES. IF YOU FINISH EARLY, YOU CAN READ A BOOK."

Yaaaasssss! Now we're talkin'.

I got right to work and smoked the first ten problems. I showed my work in detail, and wore my lead out bubbling in those answers. Then I hit a problem that stumped me.

This was the formula that Doug and I were having trouble with last week. Ugh. What was it? Maybe I'll just skip this one for now . . .

The next problem was easy. And so were the next twenty. Mr. Dooley had even thrown in a few joke questions like, What is the name of your middle school? Ha. What a joker. I breathed easy as I scratched out my work, sure that Mr. Dooley would be impressed by my first middle school test grade! I glanced up at the clock as I finished up the last problem.

I popped onto my feet, returned the sunflower pencil to the jar, and took my test and scan sheet up to Mr. Dooley.

"ARCADE! FIRST ONE TO FINISH. LOOKS LIKE YOU HAD THE LUCK OF THE SUNFLOWER WORKING IN YOUR FAVOR." Mr. Dooley winked and placed my scan sheet in the top right drawer of his desk.

"I think you're right, Mr. Dooley! I won't be surprised if I get an A . . . A for ARCADE!"

I got an F . . . F for FORGOT! It turned out that when I skipped question eleven, I *forgot* to skip a bubble! So I entered the rest of the answers in the wrong rows. Mr. Dooley had run our scan sheets during the morning break, so I got the bad news right away.

"Welcome to the fail club," Wiley Overton said to me as I tried to pass him on the way out of class. He held up his scan sheet to show me his failing grade, almost like he was proud of it. "Everyone's buzzing about how the bookworm failed the math test. How'd you do it?"

"I skipped a problem, but I forgot to skip the bubble. My answers got all off. Is that what you did?"

He scratched his head. "Nah. That would be *really* dumb! I just didn't know how to do the math. I can fix my problem with a tutor. Not sure what you can do about yours."

"I guess I need to PAY MORE ATTENTION WHEN I AM BEING TESTED."

Wiley actually laughed at my attempt to imitate Mr. Dooley. "I'm sure you'll do better next time." Then he looked down at his math book and sighed. "Math is supposed to be my *good* subject." He unzipped his huge backpack to shove the book in.

Hey, wait. Was that . . . flamingos?

I stepped in to get a closer look. Wiley quickly zipped up his pack. "Back off, bookworm, I got personal space issues."

"Sorry. I was just checking out your roomy backpack. I lost mine a couple weeks ago and this old one is ripping in spots, so I'm in the market for a new one. Do you like having such a big backpack?"

"Oh, yeah. I can carry everything in here."

"Can I see inside?"

Wiley whipped the backpack over his shoulder. "Another time. I gotta go to my next class. I think you do too." Wiley pointed up at the clock, which showed that I had two minutes to get to history.

"What's your next class, Wiley?"

"English. The worst."

"Oh. Sorry to hear that. Maybe I could help you sometime."

Wiley wiped his hands on his rumpled, brown shirt. "Not necessary. I feel like things are going to turn around for me real soon." He patted his backpack and raised an eyebrow. "See ya, Arcade."

"See ya." I headed toward the door. But Wiley didn't. Instead he walked over toward Mr. Dooley's desk. Mr. Dooley had stepped out with most of the class when the bell rang. Wiley unzipped the side pocket of his backpack and pulled out a stick. He started jamming it into the lock on the top drawer of Mr. Dooley's desk.

"I think his lock is broken, Arcade. What do you think?" He shoved the stick back in his backpack and laughed. "Yeah, things are going to turn around real soon." He pushed by me to get out the door. A bell rang.

Yeeaaah. That would be the tardy bell for history.

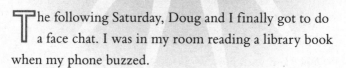

CHAPTER 22

Letter from the Past

The following Saturday, Doug and I finally got to do a face chat. I was in my room reading a library book when my phone buzzed.

"Arcade! Check this OUT!" Doug held a plastic flamingo up to his phone screen. "These ugly pink things are all over the place around here! It makes me miss Flames. How's he doin'?"

"He's okay. Getting a little bigger. And more orange."

"Hey, I got good news on the greenstone! Gram's taking it off the market for a couple months. We gotta figure out what to do with all her stuff, and right now she isn't feeling well, so she doesn't want to deal with the hassle of all the paperwork. I'm coming for a week at Thanksgiving and we'll figure it out then. I told her your family would look after the house. Is that okay?"

"Is that *okay*? Doug, that's great! I was wondering what I was going to do about Flames. I think I really should take him home."

"Home? Like to BEIJING? Dude, I wanna go this time!"

I reached down and grabbed the token in my hand. "If only I knew how to really control this thing."

"Maybe you just gotta be more specific when you talk to it. You should practice!" Doug's suggestion was a good one. What had Miss Gertrude's letter said?

I know that you have the power to control it . . .

Loopy jumped up into my lap and tried to lick the phone. "Loop! What are you doing? Now there's slobber in the cracks of the screen."

"Hey, Loopy! How ya doin', boy?" Doug waved and held up the plastic flamingo. "This is all I got for animals down here in Florida. I really miss you all, Arcade."

"We miss you too, Doug. Even Bailey—"

"Bailey Martin? I thought I stressed her out."

"Well, you do. But you also don't. Who knows with Bailey? And I could really use your help with Wiley."

Doug rubbed his eye. "You need me to take a punch for you?"

"Nah. But I think he has my flamingo backpack. I saw it poking out of his huge, brown one."

"Why would he want to keep your backpack? He doesn't seem like the flamingo type. Now a backpack with French fries on it . . . I could see that."

"That's why I'm suspicious! He also broke the lock on the top drawer of Mr. Dooley's desk. The one where he keeps all his tests and answer keys."

"Now *that's* sketchy. Hey, maybe you could use your token to find out information about Wiley."

"How would I do that?"

"Easy. You just say to it, 'Show me what's up with Wiley Overton!' Then you rub it in between your hands, like this . . ."

The token jumped on my chest and sizzled.

"Zoe would never go for it. And I promised a long time ago that I would never go anywhere with the token without her."

"She was there when he ran you over in the subway, right? I bet she'd wanna find out what that big guy is up to."

Loopy barked, jumped, and bumped the phone out of my hands. "Loop! You have no phone manners!" I dropped down on my hands and knees to pick it up. The screen was black.

"Doug?" I tapped the screen and poked a few buttons. "Doug? Aww, Loopy, did you kill the battery?"

I tossed the phone on Doug's blow-up mattress, which was still inflated next to my bed. I sat down on it and bounced.

Where would we put Doug if he came to live here permanently?

A knock sounded at my door. "Arcade?" It was Zoe.

"Yeah, come on in."

Zoe opened the door and poked her head in. "Dinner's ready in fifteen." Then she looked at me funny. "You okay?"

"I'm okay." I was about to ask her if she wanted to test the token by spying on Wiley Overton when she flung an envelope at me.

"More mail for you. You're becoming quite popular." She rushed in after the flying envelope and plopped down on the mattress. "This one looks intriguing!"

"Why?"

"Because it's from San Francisco!"

"What?" I grabbed the envelope and read my name, scrawled in messy handwriting.

"And check out the postmark."

"What's a postmark?"

"This right here!" Zoe pointed to the inked circle toward the top of the letter.

It was stamped May 27, 1937. My body went cold and my heart began to pound. I pinched the end of the envelope in my hand and ripped downward.

Zoe palmed her face. "I'm getting you a letter opener for Christmas."

I tilted the envelope and a note fell out. It was in the same messy handwriting that was on the envelope, and there were dirt smudges on the paper. I took a deep breath and read.

Dear Arcade,
The bridge is complete. All is forgiven. Come back and bring us home. You have the power to destroy us or redeem us. Choose the latter.
Sincerely,
Lenwood and Kenwood Badger

My hands started to shake. Zoe had to take the letter. "Zoe, what exactly does *redeem* mean?"

"It means to save."

"And what does *latter* mean?"

"It means they want you to pick *redeem*."

"So, do you think I really have the power to do that? And if I do, do you think I should go back for them? That would be the compassionate thing to do, right? Do you think *all* is really forgiven?"

Zoe stared down at the letter. She pushed fingers into her temple and thought a minute.

"NO! I think they're LYING! Look at this letter, Arcade! Did they even say please? Or sorry for all the trouble they caused you? And what do they mean by 'all is forgiven'? Do they think they're supposed to forgive *you* for something? YOU didn't do anything!"

"But they think I stole their token. Maybe if I go back and explain things—"

Zoe turned to me and grabbed my shoulders. "They'll take the token from you, then they'll leave you there! I'm sure that's their plan! Miss Gertrude even said not to do it! And she's their grandma! If someone's *grandma* doesn't even trust them, why should you? Nuh-uh, Arcade. You just ignore that letter. Forever. You got it?" She balled up the letter and heaved it against my wall, where it fell behind my desk.

"Kids! Time for dinner!" Mom called up the stairs. "Zoe, can you bring me a clean tablecloth from the linen closet?"

"Sure, Mom!" Zoe stood up and pointed her index finger toward my nose. "Ignore it." Then she disappeared out into the hall.

I made sure she was all the way down the stairs. Then I quietly rose and walked over to my desk. I called Loopy. "Hey, boy, can you get the ball? Come on, get the ball." I pointed to the letter that was just out of my reach. Loopy squeezed low, retrieved it, and dropped it in my hand. I petted his head. "Thanks, Loop. What would I do without you?" I lay down on the floor and smoothed out the note.

True, they didn't say sorry. And yeah, they probably want the token.

Doug's words came back into my head.

Maybe you just gotta be more specific when you talk to it. You should practice!

Maybe I should go spy on the Badgers. Then I'll know if they're telling the truth or not. But I should practice first . . . on a less threatening bully.

But how do I get Zoe to go with me?

CHAPTER 23

Spying on Wiley

"Hey, Zoe, do you love me?"

Zoe cringed. "Of course. But whatever you want, Arcade, the answer is NO."

I sat on the outside stairs of our brownstone on Sunday afternoon, playing with Loopy and munching some gummy bears, because they reminded me of Doug.

"If you love me, then why do you always argue and question my decisions?"

"Because you're an impossible noodle-head. And I want you to live a long life not embarrassing yourself in public."

I chewed and grinned. "But you'd want to be there with me, even if I made a bad decision, right? So you could protect me?"

Zoe threw her arms up in the air. "What do you want me to do now?"

I closed up my gummy bear bag and placed it on the top of the stairs. "I want you to go on a spying mission with me. Using the token. To find out what's up with Wiley Overton."

"The lumpy potato boy from the subway? Is he giving you trouble at school?"

"Not yet. But trouble's on the way. I can feel it."

"I don't think that's what you're supposed to use the token for."

"Maybe it's *exactly* what I'm supposed to use it for. I know Wiley struggles with his schoolwork. But there has to be more. Why is he so mean? Maybe I can help Wiley if I know his story. Maybe that's part of the mettle testing."

"But you still don't know how to control that thing. How do you know we won't end up on Mars or something like that?"

"Doug suggested I be more specific." The token sizzled. *Woof!*

Loopy jumped up and tried to lick the token.

I pointed to my shirt. "Did you *see* that?"

Zoe shrugged. "I *might* have seen a spark."

I pulled the token out from under my T-shirt. It was sparking all right. And gold glitter shot out toward Zoe's mouth. Loopy jumped on her lap.

I chuckled. "Nice lip gloss."

Zoe waved a finger at Loopy. "Don't you dare lick the glitter." She wiped her mouth with her sleeve. "Just how specific do you intend to be? It could be a path to disaster, Arcade."

"Every trip through the doors has been fine so far."

"Fine? Three words." Zoe held up three fingers and counted them out. "Golden. Gate. Bridge."

"Okay, that one wasn't so great. But maybe that was

the token's way of protecting us from the Badger brothers. They can't do us any harm from San Francisco, can they?" Right then, the token began to flame up around the edges. "Whoa! I think I'm on to something, here! Zoe, maybe the token is trying to protect me from Wiley Overton too!"

Zoe didn't say anything, but she was squirming there on top of those steps.

The token sputtered and pulsed and sparked and flamed. Loopy barked and wagged his tail. "Loopy's game. Are you?" I stood up and golden elevator doors appeared at the bottom of the steps.

Zoe jumped up on her feet. "This never ceases to ANNOY me, Arcade. Can't we have a peaceful Sunday afternoon? Seriously!"

I shrugged. "Who knows? Maybe this *will* be peaceful." I pulled the token off the gold chain and was about to throw it in the slot but held back instead. "I guess I better ask for something specific." I trapped the token between my palms. It was hot but, for some reason, this time it didn't burn.

Zoe adjusted her glasses and crossed her arms. "Be VERY specific, Arcade. Do you even know what specific means?"

"Of course I do. It means I need to tell it *exactly* what I want."

Zoe pulled a hair tie from her shorts pocket and put her hair in a ponytail. "That's what scares me."

"Aw, trust me, Zoe. Here we goooooo . . ." I squeezed the token in my palms. "Take us someplace . . . safe . . . where we can learn all about Wiley Overton. But—"

Zoe looked over at me. "But *what*? I see that twinkle in your eye, Arcade. You're about to make a big mista—"

"BUT don't make it boring!" I yelled. Zoe reached out to try to stop me, but she was too late. I opened my palms and the token zoomed into the coin slot. I put my hands together again, pulled them apart, and the doors opened!

Inside the elevator was a box labeled EXCITING STUFF. I reached in and discovered three cameras with head straps.

"This is DOPE! There's even a tiny one for Loopy!" I wrestled Loopy to get it on his head. He panted and slobbered all over the carpet. "Zoe, we're gonna get pictures this time. And video!" I slid the switch on the top of Loopy's camera, and a light came on. "Can't wait to see what you see, Loop!" I held one out for Zoe.

"That thing is going to look ridiculous on me."

She turned her head and put her nose up in the air.

I put mine on. "Okay, then, I guess we won't be recording this adventure from your viewpoint then."

She stuck out her hand and I gave it to her. She pulled out her ponytail, put on the camera, and then retied.

"You're right. You look ridiculous."

Adrenaline shot through my body as the elevator began to rumble and spin, like my favorite ride at the fair. The one that spins so fast it pins you to the wall and then you can lift your feet up and not fall to the ground. One time it made my cousin Derek barf and, unfortunately, that stuck to the wall too.

Ringing and squealing sounds blared from the elevator speaker. Zoe and I had to cover our ears it was so loud. Different styles of music faded in and out. The song that played the longest was the ABC song.

"This better stop spinning soon, before I bar—"

Before Zoe could say it *or* do it, the elevator came to a halt. We fell to the ground, hands grabbing our stomachs. Loopy ran around in circles, recording our reactions.

"Don't forget to turn on your camera," I said to Zoe. "Who knows, we may be bungie jumping our way out of here, and you wouldn't want to miss that."

Zoe flipped the switch on the top of her camera. "Why do I let you talk me into these things?"

We waited for what seemed like forever. Loopy barked and licked the crack between the doors. Finally, the music faded, and the doors opened.

We're in a big arena, standing on a humongous trampoline that covers the entire ground. Huge TV screens hang down, circling around us. It's kind of like Times Square, but the

TVs are a hundred times bigger. On the screens are pictures and videos of kids doing things like riding bikes, swimming, camping, crying . . . fighting . . .

Wait. It's not lots of *different* kids. It's the same kid, just at different ages! As I realize this, words begin to scroll across all the screens.

PICTURE POST . . . WILEY OVERTON . . .
PICTURE POST . . . WILEY OVERTON . . .

Woof! Woof!

Loopy's tail is wagging so fast you almost can't see it. He runs, jumps, flips over, and loses his footing on the trampoline.

I pick him up and try to calm him. "It's okay, boy." I turn to Zoe. "I think we're in Wiley's Picture Post profile on the Internet!"

"No." Zoe points to a screen that has the Picture Post guidelines listed on it. "You have to be thirteen to sign up for Picture Post. But, judging by these pictures, I'd say this is his mom's account."

Of course. This is exactly what my mom's Picture Post account looks like! My first step, my first words, my first day of school . . . my whole life's been recorded on this app.

All of a sudden, the trampoline starts to bounce us, without our help! And we can't control how high we go *or* our trajectory.

"This is CRAZY, Arcade!"

"Yeah, but it's NOT boring! Just like I ordered!" I laugh and hold Loopy tight as we fly higher with each bounce.

"Watch out, Arcade! You almost hit your head on that screen!" Zoe grits her teeth and points up at a large screen with a picture of little Wiley riding a two-wheeler with training wheels in the street.

"I can't control where I'm going!" The next time I land on the trampoline, it bounces me a little too hard. Zoe too. And when we reach the TV screen, we break right through it!

We're picking ourselves up off a sidewalk. Our head cams still have the green lights flickering.

"Wiley! That's so good! You're being brave!" A young woman stands in the middle of the street on the Upper West Side, holding her arms out to little Wiley Overton as he rides his bike toward her. "See, honey? I knew you could do it!"

Wiley jumps off the bike and hugs the woman. "Can I do it again, Mommy?"

"You bet, champ!" She helps him turn his bike around and then runs down to the other end of the street. "Okay, come on down!"

Wiley gets on his bike. A group of bigger kids are walking on the sidewalk across from us. "Hey, Wiley! You still using training wheels? Little baby! Can't you ride a bike yet?"

"Yeah! Maybe next you'll finally learn your ABCs! HAHAHAHAHA!"

"Hey! Leave him alone!" The group of kids runs away as Wiley's mom rushes back to her son. "Ignore those mean kids, Wiley. Come on. Ride your bike over to me."

We watch as Wiley starts to cry. Then he kicks his bike

over in the street. His mom comes to try to hug him, but he pushes her away, runs and grabs a rock from the gutter, and heaves it at one of the brownstones. He hits a window, breaking it.

"Whoa. That's some serious anger," Zoe says.

"And he has great aim," I add.

Wiley's mom walks over, and this time, he lets her give him a hug. "Okay, then. Let's go do the right thing." She leads him up the steps of the brownstone, and they knock at the door. A little girl about Wiley's age peeks her head out the door.

"Hello, Reagan," Wiley's mom says. "Can you please tell your parents that we're here?"

The little girl's eyes widen when she sees Wiley. "Did you just throw that rock at my window? It really scared me."

Wiley's crying a little now. "I'm sorry, Reagan."

She says nothing to Wiley but, instead, turns and yells into the house, "Mom! Dad! Whiny Overton is here! And guess what? He broke ANOTHER window!"

Next thing we know we're being pulled out of this screen. It's like a giant vacuum has attached itself to our feet. We land back inside the arena on the trampoline. But we don't stay long, because we're bounced again until we crash through another Picture Post!

Now we're at a school, crouching behind bushes, witnessing an argument. Wiley Overton's a little older now, and he's holding a poster, shaking his fist at a group of boys. "Who put this up? I'm gonna blast ya!"

The boys laugh and try to walk away. Wiley follows and grabs one by the shoulders. He pulls him down on the concrete.

"Back off, Wiley! We didn't put it up there. We couldn't care less if it's third grade and you CAN'T READ YET." They all laugh again. Wiley drops the poster and starts to punch away on the kid. Whistles blow and a couple of teachers come running over to break up the fight. There's a bunch of yelling and pointing of fingers, which ends with one of the teachers leading Wiley and two of the boys into the building.

The wind whips up and blows the poster in our direction. Zoe picks it up, and then covers her mouth with her hand. "This is terrible!" She turns it so I can see.

WHINY OVERTON–DUMBEST KID IN THIRD GRADE

There's a drawing on the poster. The person didn't have great art skills, but I can tell it's Wiley's face.

I take the poster from Zoe, fold it up, and put it in my pocket. Right then, the vacuum sucks us back to the trampoline, where we're bounced around in a tornado of golden glitter.

"OKAY, I'm ready for boring now!" I yell. The token returns to the chain on my neck, and one of the huge screens turns from Wiley's mom's Picture Post account to a pair of golden elevator doors.

Whew!

"Watch this, Zoe!" I grab my token off the chain and flip it with my thumb to see if it will land in the coin slot. "Whoop! Three-point shot!"

Cousin Derek would be proud.

Zoe brushes glitter from her shorts inside the elevator and pulls the head cam off so she can smooth her hair. "Do you think we should leave these here?"

I take the camera from her and pull out the memory card. 'Yes, but we'll take these. We can download the files to our laptops. Should be some pretty sweet footage!" I take off my camera, retrieve the card, and put it back in the box labeled EXCITING STUFF.

"Okay, Loop, time to get that silly thing off your head." I look around. "Loop?"

The elevator doors opened at the bottom of our brownstone steps. Usually this is when I feel relieved and refreshed, and sometimes a little confused. But this time, I was horrified.

"WHERE'S LOOPY? Is he hiding? ZOE, help me find him!!!"

Zoe and I checked every square inch of the elevator. No Loopy.

"I think we should stay in here, Arcade. Maybe the doors will close and we can go back and get him."

I put the token between my palms and spoke SPECIFICALLY: "Take us back so we can get Loopy!" But there was no heat. No sparks. No glitter. And then, as if to rub it in my face, the elevator tilted, dumping Zoe and me out at the bottom of our brownstone steps.

"NOOOOOO! Take me back to Loopy! Bring my dog back!" I reached for the token and tried to wrestle it off the chain. Zoe grabbed my hands.

"Arcade, STOP! People are walking by. You need to calm down."

"I CAN'T CALM DOWN. LOOPY'S GONE!"

"Please, Arcade. Come up here and sit down. I'll help you figure this out. We'll find him."

I covered my face with my hands. Zoe pulled them down. "We'll FIND him."

And then, along came Michael Tolley. "Hey, everyone! How's it going?" Michael took one look at me and ran up the stairs. "Arcade, what's going on? Are you sick?"

I couldn't stop my hands from shaking. Sweat squirted out of every pore of my body. I felt sick to my stomach. Tears ran down my cheeks.

"We lost Loopy," Zoe said, and a few tears ran down her cheeks too.

"Your cute little dog? Oh, no!" Michael grabbed the back of his neck. "When did you last see him?"

"I don't know." I threw my hands up in defeat.

Was it at Wiley's house when he was riding his bike? Or Wiley's school when he was in third grade? Did Loopy even make it to the school?

"He was here with us on the steps a few minutes ago," Zoe said. "Then we . . . got a little distracted."

Michael grinned. "Well, he couldn't have made it very far then. I'll help you find him. I bet he took off toward the park. Dogs love the park."

I wish it were that simple.

Michael took his phone out of his pocket and started texting. "I'll get my brothers to search. They need something constructive to do. I've got a few other friends who can help too. Do you have a picture of Loopy I can send them? Also, does he have a collar or a leash attached or anything that would make him stand out?"

"This is going to sound funny," Zoe said, "but he had one of those head cams on."

"A what?"

"A head camera. You know, so you can take action pics and video without using your hands. They work really well for dogs." She grinned a little.

"Okay, then, this should be NOOOO problem." Michael poked away on his phone for a few seconds and then looked up at us. "I'm ready to start looking if you are." He gave Zoe a gentle smile. "Should we divide and conquer, or do this together?"

Right then, my friends Scratchy and Carlos came wheeling by. "What's up, Dude?" Scratchy asked.

"We lost Loopy," Zoe said. "Do you want to help us find him?"

"Who's Loopy?" Carlos wheeled his chair in closer to us.

I pulled out my phone and showed him a picture of my little pooch. "He disappeared from, uh . . . the porch here." I gave a sly glance over to Scratchy, who's been with me on a couple of token adventures. He pointed to my chest, and I nodded.

"Dude. That's NOT RAD."

"Well, hey," Carlos grabbed tight to the arms of his wheelchair, "I'm fast in this thing. And I know the park really well. You think he ran over there?"

"Maybe."

He's not there.

"Okay, we'll find him!" Carlos revved up his wheelchair. "Scratchy's been helping me soup this thing up. This will be a great test!"

Always pay attention when you are being tested.

"I'll go tell Mom and Dad where we're going." Zoe said. She must have seen the look of terror in my eyes. "What?"

"Don't tell them about Loopy yet. Let's see if he turns up first."

Arcade! Thanks for calling me, man! I'm SOOO bored here in Florida! What's up?" I held the phone tightly to my ear as we ran over to Central Park.

"Doug! Loopy's lost!"

"Loopy's LOST? OH, NO! Where'd you lose him?"

"In the doors."

"The doors?"

"The elevator doors. We were in the Internet . . ."

"Did you just say you were *in* the Internet?"

"Yeah. Well, only the Picture Post app."

"Oh. That's CRAZY COOL!"

"Yeah, it is. I mean it was. Until Loopy disappeared."

I had to take a break to catch my breath. Michael and Zoe were two blocks ahead of me and were getting ready to cross the street into Central Park. "Doug, I have an important question for you."

"Well, shoot, bro! What is it?"

"Do you remember what street Wiley Overton lived on when he was in first or second grade?"

"Why? Did Wiley take Loopy?"

"No. But we were at Wiley's house when he was little the last time I saw him. I think. Anyway, do you remember, Doug?"

Doug was quiet for a few seconds. "I'm sorry, Arcade. I don't know. But I know I could walk there from my house."

"Really? Which direction? North or south?"

"North or south? Who knows? I didn't have good direction then. I don't really have it now. Good thing everything in New York City is numbered! Even the schools . . ."

"That's it! The schools! What school did Wiley go to in third grade?"

"You know where he went, bro. He went to PS 23. Before he got kicked out, I mean."

"PS 23? Right! That makes sense. Doug, I gotta go. I'm sorry!"

"No worries. Go find Loopy. Hey, have you talked to your parents about adopting me, yet?"

I kicked myself on the inside. "No, I haven't had time to have a serious conversation with them yet. But I will. I promise."

Doug sighed. "Okay. Well, go find your little pooch . . . And shoot me a text when you do!"

"I will. Thanks, Doug!" I stopped to put my phone in my back pocket. "ZOE! I'm going to PS 23!"

Zoe turned around. "What? Not by yourself you're not. I'm going with you!"

Zoe ran back to me, and Michael followed. "I'll hang with you two. Let Carlos and Scratchy ride through the park. With their wheels they'll be faster. Why do you want to go to PS 23?"

"Uh, I just got a tip that Loopy might be there."

"Okay then, let's go!" Michael changed direction and started jogging west. Zoe waited until he was out of hearing range before whispering to me, "I don't know if Loopy made it to the school scene, Arcade. I was too busy watching the boys fight to notice. And who knows if it's even possible to find him if we don't go through the doors first."

"I know. But we gotta check. He's my dog!"

Zoe's shoulders rose, then fell. "I know. Let's go."

It took us about twenty minutes to get to PS 23. The gates were locked around the small yard outside the building. Michael jumped up, threw his leg over the chain-link fence, and dropped himself inside. "I'll go check it out!" He disappeared behind the far wall.

I peered through the metal fence, hoping to spot the place where Wiley had his fight with the boys in third grade. "It has to be . . . THERE! Those are the bushes we hid behind."

Zoe grabbed the fence and pushed her nose through a gap. "I don't see him, Arcade. And Loopy's fast. I can't imagine he'd stay put."

"He would if he was waiting for me."

Zoe's phone buzzed, and she jumped, letting go of the fence. "Maybe Michael found something." She unlocked the screen with her thumb and her eyes popped wide open. "Arcaaaaade . . . you'll want to take a look at THIS."

"What?" I jumped over next to Zoe. She poked a couple more buttons on her screen.

"I'm getting some notifications."

"What kind of notifications?"

She turned the phone my way. "From my Picture Post app. I have a new follower."

"Is that good?"

Zoe put her hand on her hip. "Here. I clicked on his profile. You tell me."

I pulled the phone in close to look. A familiar face filled the screen, but I couldn't believe my eyes. "This is impossible!"

"Oh, yeah? I'm surprised to hear you say that, Mr. My-Token-Can-Do-Anything."

The new follower's username was @LoopDogNYC. And the profile picture was . . . LOOPY! With his tongue sticking out, his ears perked, and his head cam on!

"Follow him back, Zoe!" I handed the phone over to her, and she clicked "follow."

"Oh, this is funny," Zoe said.

"What?"

"Loopy posted his first picture! I think we're barking up the wrong tree, Arcade. Check this out. This picture was posted five minutes ago."

It had to be a picture taken from his head cam. It showed his front, furry legs running, and in the distance was a bridge I had seen before. In Central Park.

"Zoe! That's the Bow Bridge!"

"hat's over by the Ramble," Zoe said. "Let's go!" We both tore out of there.

I pulled my phone out of my pocket. "I'll tell Scratchy and Carlos. Maybe they're over there now." My fingers shook as I pulled up the number and called Scratchy.

"Hey, Arcade!" I could hear the buzz of Scratchy's scooter in the background. "Did you find him?"

"Nah, but we saw a pos—I mean, he's been spotted heading toward the Bow Bridge."

"That's RADICAL! We're in the Ramble right now. We'll head over there." I could hear Scratchy turn off his scooter and yell, "CJ! Turn your wheels around. He's this way!"

"We're on our way back from PS 23," I said. "We'll be there as soon as we can."

"And we'll let you know when we have him!" Scratchy hung up and I clicked off the phone. I took a second to catch my breath.

Thank goodness for friends with wheels.

The Bow Bridge is one of the most famous landmarks in Central Park. They call it Bow because it's bent like an archer's or violinist's bow. I knew that from reading *New York City: A Coffee Table Tour.*

"I gotta get some water," Zoe said as we ran by a corner store across from the park. I followed her through some revolving doors that led inside. It took her only seconds to grab a bottle of water from the cooler, but then we had to wait in a long line.

"Maybe I should run ahead and have you catch up," I said.

"NO. You stay right here, little bro."

"But Loopy's fast, Zoe."

"Yeah, I know. And you have friends out looking for him. Plus, we don't know if he's at the Bow Bridge *now*, or if he's at the Bow Bridge *in the past.*"

I scratched my head. "Huh?"

Zoe cracked open the water and took a sip. Then she offered me some. "Yeah, I know. Confusing, isn't it?"

After a few minutes, we finally made it up to the cashier. By then, I had added another water bottle to our order.

"Time's getting short, Arcade. Mom's gonna want us home for dinner in a couple of hours."

"No worries. I'm sure we'll find him by then. Come on!"

We ran across the street, into the park, and Zoe's phone buzzed again. Her eyes bugged out of her head when she looked at the text. "OH, NO! It's Michael!"

"Michael who?"

Zoe smacked me on the back of the head. "Michael Tolley! We left him at the school!"

I stopped running, grabbed my stomach, and laughed. "Oh, dude! I totally forgot! And *you* ditched him! He'll never date you now."

Zoe stood there, glaring, with her hand on her hip and her chin in the air. "That's NOT funny, Arcade."

"I'm sorry. He'll forgive you." I stopped laughing. I really did feel bad. Michael's a nice guy. He didn't deserve to be ditched. Not by his current Broadway "girlfriend," Trista, not by me, and definitely not by his hope-to-be-in-the-near-future girlfriend, Zoe.

"Mom, hey, Arcade and I are at the park. We're going to hang out in the Ramble for a bit." Zoe talked on her phone as she race-walked with me on the main road that runs along the edge of the park. "Yes . . . I know . . . we're watching out for each other. Yes, I'm working on my goal. Okay . . . yes. Five-thirty for dinner. Gotcha." She clicked her phone off. "We have an hour and a half. That's it for today."

We took off down some winding paths, heading through the Ramble toward the Bow Bridge.

"Maybe Loopy came in here and he's resting on a bench or something. Any new notifications from Picture Post?"

Zoe looked at her phone. "Nothing from @LoopDogNYC."

We ran by another bench, and there sat our pedicab driver friend, Elijah. "Hello, friends! It is wonderful to see

you again. Are you searching for the hidden cave, Arcade?"
Elijah did not have his pedicab with him.

I sat down next to him to catch my breath and drink a
little more water. "Is this your thinking day, Elijah?"

He nodded. "Oh, yes. It has been so peaceful. Have you
found your backpack?"

"Maybe. I thought I saw it a couple of days ago, inside
the guy's backpack who stole it from me. I have to think of a
way to get it back without getting a black eye."

Elijah nodded. "I see. Well, you are a creative young
lad. I am sure you will come up with the perfect solution
that will be safe for everyone."

"I sure hope so. Hey, Elijah, did you by any chance see a
little chocolate-colored shih-poo with a head cam run by here?"

He shook his head. "A head cam? I sure would not have
missed that. Is he your dog?"

I sighed. "Yep. He ran off. And he was spotted over by
the Bow Bridge. We're headed there now."

"Oh, I am so sorry he's lost. My, you seem to be going
through a few fiery trials of late."

My token surged. "Fiery trials?"

"Yes. You had your backpack stolen. And now your dog
is missing?"

"And his best friend," Zoe added.

"Your friend is missing?"

"No. He moved." I said. "To Florida."

"Oh." Elijah nodded again. "I am so sorry, Arcade.
Sometimes trials come all at once."

"You're telling me."

"It feels horrible, but I was just reading that when that happens, we can rejoice, because trials help us build endurance and strength of character."

"Yeah," Zoe said. "I've been telling Arcade that his mettle is being tested."

"Mettle? That is a complicated word."

"I'm finding that out." I slumped down on the bench.

Elijah leaned forward. "Well, I will be sure to keep an eye out for a flamingo backpack and a little dog with a head cam." He pulled out a paper from his book and scribbled on it. "Here is my phone number. Call me if you would like the use of my pedicab for your search. No charge."

I took the paper. "Thanks, Elijah. You're the best."

I shook his hand, and he rested back on his bench while Zoe and I took off toward the Bow Bridge. And for some reason, I didn't feel as panicked as before.

"I like Elijah," I said. "He's peaceful."

"Yeah. I think it's the Ramble." Zoe gazed up in the trees and watched a few birds flitting around.

"No, I think it's him. He's always like that."

My phone rang. It was Scratchy.

"Hey, Arcade, Carlos and I have been all over the area around Bow Bridge. No sign of Loopy. I'm sorry, man. Is there anywhere else you'd like us to look?"

"Where are you now?"

"We're at that little café a few blocks south of the lake. Picking up a snack."

"Okay. Hang tight. We'll see you in a few minutes."

When we got to the café, Carlos and Scratchy were eating muffins and feeding crumbs to tiny birds at their table.

"We've been all over," Scratchy said. "You should see how fast Carlos gets around here."

I patted Carlos on the shoulder. "Thanks, man."

"You're welcome! It's fun to help. I just wish we had found him. We asked a bunch of people too. No one saw a little dog with a head cam."

Zoe checked her phone.

"Any new notifications?" I asked.

"No. And it's going to take us a little while to get home. I say we head back and try this again another time."

"But tomorrow's school," I said. "I don't think I can stand it knowing he'll be out here all night somewhere, lost."

"We'll come help you search tomorrow after school," Scratchy said. "You never know, maybe he'll even find his way to your front door. You hear about that happening with dogs all the time."

But I lost him in the Internet. And you never hear about that.

"Thanks a lot, you guys." Zoe aimed her phone at the little birds eating the muffins and took a picture. "I'm sure you need to be getting home too. Arcade will keep you posted on the search."

Scratchy wiped muffin crumbs off his lap and jumped up on his scooter. "Okay, we'll take some of the curvy paths home and let you know if we see him. You up for that, Carlos?"

Carlos leaned back and popped a wheelie. "Sure! I can navigate a few bumps."

And with that, Scratchy and Carlos zoomed off.

"I guess we should tell Mom and Dad." I hung my head as we approached the stairway to our brownstone. "I mean, it's not like they aren't gonna notice that Loopy's gone."

Zoe nodded. "Yeah. But what *exactly* are we going to tell them?"

"Hey, you two! How was the park?" Dad came in from the back porch carrying barbequed steak on a platter. "Are you hungry?"

"The park was lovely," Zoe said. "But we have some bad news to tell you. It might ruin your appetite."

"Oh?" Mom came out from the kitchen, carrying iced teas that she set on the dining room table. "Is someone hurt? Sick?" She gave us each a once-over.

I decided to just spill it. "We lost Loopy."

Mom put both hands up to her mouth. "Oh, dear!"

I sat down and took a sip of tea. "We've been looking all afternoon. Our friends have been too."

Dad frowned. "Why didn't you tell us right away? We could have helped you look."

"We didn't want to worry you," Zoe said. "Plus, we kept thinking he'd show up somewhere, any minute. You know Loopy. And then the minutes turned to hours—"

"And then we were in the Ramble . . ." I chimed in.

Dad put the platter of steaks on the dinner table. "Okay, this is what we'll do. We'll eat and then we'll print out some signs. Then we'll take a walk and hang them up all over the neighborhood. Someone's sure to have seen him." He turned to Mom. "Is everything else ready?"

"You bet. Mashed potatoes, salad, and a special tonight . . . shrimp cocktail!"

"Wow, fancy!" Dad said.

And perfect timing! We're running out of food for Flames.

Zoe and I did our best to sneak as many shrimps as we could into our napkins. Thankfully, Dad and Mom were distracted by our Loopy news, so they spent a lot of time discussing possible solutions with each other.

"We can put Loopy's picture on social media too," Mom said. "There's the neighborhood page and, even better, I'll put it on my Picture Post account!"

"All that is good," Dad said. Then he looked at me. "How're you doing, bud? Don't give up hope. We'll find him."

I nodded and tried to swallow my bite of steak through the lump in my throat. "I know. I'm just worried."

"Of course, you are. He's your dog. And he's lost. That's normal."

"I'm worried about Doug too."

"Oh? And how is Doug doing at his aunt's house? We sure miss him around here."

"Yeah, me too. He's doing okay. But he could be better. I have an idea how we could help him."

Dad put down his fork. Mom did too.

"Go on . . ." Dad said.

"Well, if he lives in Florida, he can't see his grandma. She raised him, you know."

"Yes," Mom said. "He must miss her terribly." Both my parents stared at me. I watched out of the corner of my eye as Zoe took the opportunity to shovel the rest of the shrimp into her napkin.

"And I think it would be better for Doug's grandma if she could see him more often."

"Those are some good thoughts, Arcade."

"Yeah. Compassionate," Zoe added.

I sat up straighter and wiped my mouth with my napkin. "Yes, so I was wondering if we could look into adopting Doug."

Silence.

Dad put his elbows on the table and clasped his hands together. He rested his chin on his hands. "Wow. That's a serious request."

"Yes, it is." Mom stared at Dad.

"That would change the dynamics of this family forever."

"It would definitely add to the food bill," Zoe said. "And it would give me *another* pesky little brother."

"We'd have to take some time to pray about it, and we don't even know if it's possible to adopt Doug if his aunt wants to keep him." Mom pulled her napkin off her lap and began to fold it on the table.

I balled up my napkin and threw it on my plate. "And why does SHE get to choose? Shouldn't it be up to Doug?" I covered my heart with my hand. The token was resting over it. "I'm sorry. It's been a horrible afternoon, and I'm REALLY worried about Loopy."

I don't usually leave the table without permission, but I had to get out of there. I pushed back in my chair and ran up the stairs to my room, half slamming the door. I flopped down on my bed and punched my pillow a whole bunch of times until I got tired.

Okay, token. You can stop the testing now. I'm pretty sure I'm NOT the right kid.

I rolled over, sat up, and ripped the chain and the token off my neck. I pulled open my top drawer, the one that holds my underwear, and I threw it in. "You're better off with the Badger brothers."

There was a knock at the door. I didn't answer, but Zoe barged in anyway.

"I didn't say come in."

She crossed her arms and stared at my neck. "Where's the token?"

I pointed to my drawer. She walked over, opened it, fished around, and pulled it out. She held out the chain. The token spun around and around. "That's not the answer, and you know it."

"I'm tired of all this, Zoe! I'm NOT the right kid! I'm not worthy to wear pure gold. I'm failing *all* the tests. Oh, and by the way, I failed a test at school too. So why bother?"

"Why *bother*? You're just going to give up *that* easy? Do

you have any *mettle* at all? Don't you remember what Elijah said today? About fiery trials?"

I shrugged. "He said they produce strength and character."

"And he should know! He didn't have the greatest life before he came to New York City, and it's not that easy for him still. And yet he's strong through it all. And you said it yourself this afternoon. He's peaceful."

"But he's older than me," I said. "He can handle it better."

"Okay, how about Doug and all he's going through? How about Wiley? Can they run away from their trials? What about *Carlos*? Can he throw his wheelchair in his underwear drawer and be done with it? They can't quit their trials, and you shouldn't either."

I wanted to argue with her soooo bad. Show her how her point-of-view was way off. I'm usually so good at that! But this time, as much as I hated to admit it, Zoe was r . . . Zoe was ri . . . okay, Zoe was right.

I reached out, snatched the chain from her hand, and draped it over my neck.

Zoe smiled. "That's better. We both have a lot to learn about that token of yours, but we'll figure it out together. And we'll get Loopy back. Doug's home is here in New York, so we'll get him back too. And you're going to find your backpack. Or we'll fail together, knowing we gave everything we had, without ever giving up."

"What about my library book?"

Zoe rolled her eyes. "Your library book? Seriously?

Don't you EVEN THINK of going back to the Gold Rush. I'll pay your replacement fee."

I nodded. "Deal."

Zoe walked over to the door. "So, do you want to go for a walk with the family? Mom is printing out hundreds of 'Lost Dog' signs right now."

I scooted off the bed. "Sure."

"And after that, we'll sneak over to Doug's and feed Flames. I got a napkin load of shrimp for him." Zoe wiggled her eyebrows up and down. "SQUAWK!"

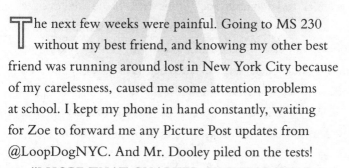

CHAPTER 28
Waiting
and
Watching

The next few weeks were painful. Going to MS 230 without my best friend, and knowing my other best friend was running around lost in New York City because of my carelessness, caused me some attention problems at school. I kept my phone in hand constantly, waiting for Zoe to forward me any Picture Post updates from @LoopDogNYC. And Mr. Dooley piled on the tests!

"I HOPE THAT CHAPTER FIVE HAS STUCK IN YOUR BRAINS," Mr. Dooley said as he handed out another computer scan sheet. "YOU HAVE FORTY-FIVE MINUTES. DO NOT SKIP BUBBLES, PEOPLE!" Mr. Dooley came by my desk and spied the phone sitting on the corner. "Put that away, Mr. Livingston. I don't consider you the cheating type, but you don't want to give me any reason to doubt you."

I grabbed my phone, checking it one more time for news of Loopy. Nothing. I shoved it in my old, multicolored backpack.

Mr. Dooley walked back to his desk and fiddled with the

broken top-drawer lock. I glanced over at Wiley Overton, who was filling in bubbles like crazy. He took a paper out of his notebook and slipped it under his test. I looked around at the rest of the class. Bailey was working diligently, while chewing her eraser down to nothing. Carlos smiled away and flipped his hair while he worked. Amber Lin, my friend who had been with me on an adventure through the doors to a veterinary clinic, was ultra-focused, just like she had been when we operated on Samson, the police K-9. Scratchy used his pencil to scratch the back of his neck. He looked over at me, crossed his eyes, and stuck out his tongue, making me chuckle under my breath. And the Tolleys—they had papers hiding under their tests too, and they slid them out and back several times while they worked.

"ARCADE, CAN YOU PLEASE COME UP HERE?"

Mr. Dooley was looking right at me, curling his index finger.

"Um . . . yes, sir." I scooted out of my chair and walked up to his desk.

"Arcade, is something wrong? You seem very distracted today. Is this test too hard?"

They're all too hard.

"No, sir. I'm sorry. I'll try to focus better."

"Look, I know it's been hard for you since Doug moved . . ."

When he said that, a bolt of heat shot from my token.

". . . and middle school is a lot harder than elementary school."

"Yes, it is."

"But you're still Arcade Livingston! You have all the same interests and talents and great character traits that you had last year. The world needs more caring people like you, so don't let the challenges and setbacks throw you off track, okay? Keep digging in."

"Okay. Thanks, Mr. Dooley." I turned and walked back through the middle of the classroom. On my way, I spotted even more kids with extra papers under their tests!

"What's with the extra paper," I whispered to one of the Tolleys.

He tapped his pencil on his desk. "Scratch paper."

I returned to my desk in the back row. We had twenty minutes left of test time. Wiley Overton got up and turned his paper in.

That's odd.

"Thank you, Wiley," Mr. Dooley said. "You may read a book now." Wiley went back to his desk and, instead of pulling out a book to read, he brought out a sketch pad and some drawing pencils.

The Tolleys finished way before me too. In fact, half the class seemed to finish at about the same time, leaving Bailey, Amber, Carlos, Scratchy, and me working away until the break bell.

When I turned my test in on my way out, Mr. Dooley was playing with the lock on his desk drawer. "There's bark in it or something," I heard him say to himself. Then he looked up at me and reached out to take my test. "Mr. Livingston, make sure to stop by my office before you leave school today. My brother Patrick sent a package for you."

"Patrick? From the Empire Fish Market?"

"Precisely. He told me that you and your friends LOVE shrimp. He found that quirky, yet refreshing, so he sent you a ten-pound bag."

The next day, we got our tests back. I got a C plus. Not my best work. But I didn't study nearly as much as I could have. Instead, the night before, I got distracted reading a book from the library about foster adoption.

"SOME OF YOU EXCELLED ON THIS TEST, WHILE OTHERS . . ." Mr. Dooley hung his head and pretended to cry, ". . . WILL NEED TO MAKE STUDYING A PRIORITY NEXT TIME."

The bell rang for the next period. I gathered my things up to leave. As I passed desks, I saw multiple As written on the top of people's scan sheets. There were even As on the Tolleys's tests!

"Hey, Scratch, what did you get on the math test?"

He held his test up for me to see. "B plus. There were a couple of stumpers on here." Of all the kids I know, Scratchy is the best at math, so the fact that the Tolleys beat him had *me* scratching my head.

Something's up.

I summoned a bit of courage and walked over to Wiley on my way out. "Hey, Wiley."

He tipped his head to me. "Yeah?"

"How'd you do on the math test?"

"I did pretty good." He held it up so I could see. It was an A minus. "How about you?"

"C plus. Guess I need to make studying a priority."

Wiley gave me a funny stare. "Maybe. Maybe not. You gotta do what works to get through, you know?" Then he patted his backpack and walked out the door.

CHAPTER 29

Flamingos Everywhere!

"Doug, I think there's a cheating ring going on at school." Doug and I were having our weekly face chat while I sat outside my house on that chilly October afternoon.

"You think there's a cheating ring going on at school?"

"Yeah, dude. That's what I said."

"Who's smart enough to run a cheating ring? And if they're *that* smart, why cheat?" Doug munched away on some potato chips as he talked. "Any news on your family adopting me? My aunt follows me around the house with a vacuum all the time."

I laughed. "Well, you do leave a trail of crumbs wherever you go. I've been reading up on adoption, and my parents are still thinking about it. They called your social worker so they can get more information. They have an appointment in a couple of weeks to talk about options."

"A couple of weeks? I don't think I can take it much longer."

I touched my token and remembered Zoe's speech about

staying strong when all I wanted to do was run and hide. "Yes, you can. This trial will build your character."

"But my gram called. She's really sick this time. Arcade, what if she . . . you know. What if I don't get a chance to see her again?"

"I'll see what I can do to speed things up."

"Thanks, Arcade. Have you gone anywhere cool with your token lately?"

"Nope. I think it's punishing me for losing Loopy."

"Hey, the Loopster is out there, and he'll find you. He's cool like that."

"I hope."

"How's Flames?"

"He's getting bigger and messier. I've tried a couple times to take him outside, but he starts squawking, and I have to bring him in. And we might have to repaint your bathroom. I'll spare you the gross details."

"You should take him to the Ramble. Lots of squawking out there with those birds. No one would notice."

"That's an adventurous idea. I'll run it by Zoe. Her fun goal was to watch birds in the Ramble. Ha! She could flamingo-sit."

"Something tells me that's NOT what Zoe meant."

"True. But that *is* what she *said*."

On Monday, I spotted my flamingo backpack at school! At least it looked a lot like mine. It was hanging on the shoulder of a kid named Aiden Pickett. He wasn't in my homeroom, but I knew he had Dooley for math class because I saw him there the day I went in after school to pick up the shrimp packet.

I decided to do a little digging. I ran up to Aiden. "Hey."

"Hey. You're name's Arcade, right?"

I smiled. "That's me."

He nodded. "Cool. I want to thank you for making MS 230 a much better place to be."

"Uh, thanks. I guess. I mean, have we met before?"

He shook his head. "No. But everyone knows *you*. You like to help people. And you're really making a difference here." Aiden waved to a buddy across the hall. "Hey, Preston! Wait up!" Then he looked back at me. "See ya, Arcade! Keep up the good work!" Then he laughed and sped off, the flamingo backpack jumping up and down as he ran.

On Tuesday, I saw the backpack again! It was sitting in the middle of a girls' lunch table. I walked up to get a closer look. "Hi, Arcade." They started to giggle. "You're the bomb," one of them said.

Awkward!

I got out of there fast!

On Wednesday *and* Thursday, I watched as the backpack skipped around to other groups on campus.

Is there a new flamingo backpack fad that everyone knows about but me?

Something smelled . . . shrimpy.

Reagan Cooper, who was assigned to another homeroom, walked up next to me, crossed her arms, and glared at a couple of boys who sat on the grass, next to a flamingo backpack.

She narrowed her eyes. "They're ALL cheaters, Arcade."

"Cheaters?"

She tapped her foot. "Yeah. And it's about time they got busted." Then she stomped off.

CHAPTER 30

The Crown

The late October air turned cold, so I dug out my warm hoodie for the Thursday morning walk to school. As soon as I stepped outside, I regretted wearing shorts.

"Brrrr! It hasn't been this cold since we moved here," I said to Zoe, who was texting Michael Tolley to see if he wanted to ride the subway with her to school that morning.

I looked over her shoulder. "Anything from Loopy?"

"No. I'm sorry, Arcade."

We had been searching high and low for Loopy every day after school for a month. Scratchy and Carlos had driven miles in the park, even over to the Upper East Side. Zoe and I had walked all the Upper West Side neighborhoods between Central Park and Riverside Park. We had even downloaded the files from the memory cards we took out of our head cams the day Loopy disappeared. All we found were the same scenes we both saw that day. Wiley throwing a rock, Wiley punching some kids, and then . . . nothing.

Zoe pulled her thick, pink, cable-knit sweater up to

cover her neck from the wind. "But check this out. He's gaining followers." She handed me her phone.

"How did he get 435 followers?"

"Who knows? You have a weird dog. People follow weird." She grinned. "But at least we know he's still out there, right?"

Right then, Carlos and Scratchy came rolling by. "Hey, we thought we'd come down your street and see if you wanted a ride to school. Wanna climb on back?" Scratchy pointed his thumb over his shoulder.

"Sure!" I ran down the steps of our brownstone and got ready to ride with Scratchy.

"Hey! Wait ONE minute!" Zoe put her hand out. "There's a new post! But . . . this can't be!"

"What can't be?" I motioned for Carlos and Scratchy to wait a minute and I ran back up the steps to look at Zoe's phone. @LoopDogNYC had posted two new pictures! It was his furry legs all right, and they were running up some stairs. I swiped to the next picture. It was a sign hanging on a wall, with a drawing of the Statue of Liberty. Next to the drawing it said "128 steps to the top of the Pedestal!"

"Loopy's on Liberty Island!" I yelled down to my friends.

"WHAT? That's RAD! Let's go get him!"

"You bet!" I yelled.

"Arcade, you can't! You have school."

"But Zoe, he's been gone for a month!"

"I know, but you just can't skip schoo—"

Just then the fiery metal tester hanging around my neck sizzled into action.

Orange glitter swirled down from the trees that had begun changing into their fall colors, and it fell on our shoulders. Carlos brushed some off with his hand. "What is *this* stuff? I've lived in New York City my whole life. We've *never* had orange snow before."

Scratchy's eyes popped out of his head. "Oh, man! Arcade! Are we going traveling? Anything but a plane, buddy! Anything but a plane!" He laughed.

I thought of the time Scratchy traveled with me through the elevator doors and he ended up having to fly a plane over the Statue of Liberty.

"Traveling?" Carlos asked. "Where are we going? I'll get my handicap access map."

"You won't need it where we're going, Carlos. We're totally skipping the subway." He looked confused as I pulled the now scorching Triple T Token out from under my shirt. A few flames shot out from the middle.

"What IS THAT?" Carlos's eyes were fixed on my chest.

Zoe came down from the steps. "It's a little thing that causes a whole lot of trouble."

"She means *excitement*," I said. "And I think we're gonna get Loopy back today!" Golden elevator doors rose from the sidewalk at the bottom of our brownstone steps.

"Here's the portable elevator you've always wanted, Carlos."

Carlos's jaw dropped open.

I pulled the token from the chain and clasped it between my palms.

Remember to be specific.

"Take us to the pedestal of the Statue of Liberty . . ." I began, glancing over at Carlos, who was looking down at his wheels, concern all over his face, ". . . and let Carlos go *everywhere* we go."

A golden coin slot, shaped like the Statue of Liberty's torch, rose up from the ground, right in front of the doors. I flipped the token up into the air. It turned around and around before finding its way like it always did into the slot. I pulled my hands apart. The doors opened.

"Here we go!" I yelled. "This is better than the subway elevators, Carlos. I promise!"

"RADICAL!" Scratchy revved his scooter and rode it in.

"You're going to freeze in those shorts, Arcade!" Zoe wrapped herself up in her puffy jacket and stepped in.

But Carlos held up. "You know we . . . uhhh . . . got a . . . uhhh . . . a test in Dooley's today, right?"

I swiped a hand in the air. "No worries. We'll be back in plenty of time. Come on, this will be fun." I ran over behind Carlos's chair and pushed him in.

"My phone still works, for now." Zoe said. "Look! He's posted *another* picture." She showed it to me. It was a different sign. This time it said "67 steps to the top of the Pedestal."

"Here's a Statue of Liberty fact, you guys." I read the

small print on the sign in Loopy's post. "In very strong winds, the Statue of Liberty can sway three inches, while her torch can sway almost six inches."

"Let's hope it's not windy then," Zoe said, snatching her phone back.

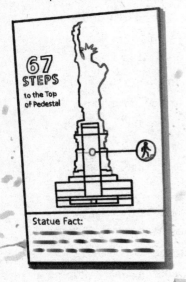

67
STEPS
to the Top
of Pedestal

Statue Fact:

The elevator stayed still this time, but loud sloshing sounds came blaring from the speakers. Then a horn. It sounded low and long, like it was coming from a ferry.

"Water! Nice," Carlos said. "I like to swim."

But I asked for the pedestal. Please let us be on the pedestal when this thing opens.

Ding!

I closed my eyes.

"We made it, Arcade! Whatever you said did the trick!" Zoe runs from the elevator, looking . . . a little younger?

We're not on the pedestal . . . we're *in* the pedestal. "I think it's through those doors," I say as I lead the group out of the elevator. I turn to Scratchy. "You better leave your wheels here." Scratchy nods.

And then something crazy happens. Carlos must think I'm talking to him, because he STANDS UP and says, "OKAY!"

"WHAT DID YOU JUST DO, CARLOS!?!" The shock of what I'm seeing has me talking like Dooley.

Carlos is standing there, his mouth wide open, his arms in the air. "What's going on, Arcade? This is UNBELIEVABLE!" His voice is a little higher and less crackly than it was a few minutes ago.

"Arcade! Look at us!" Scratchy examines his arms and then wraps his fingers around his upper leg. "We shrunk or something."

I jump up and down a little. Yeah, I'm lighter and quicker! Am I younger?

Zoe runs back in the elevator to get us. "Are you guys coming? Loopy's not going to wait arou—" She looks at me and Scratchy and starts to laugh. "You're little kids again! This is hilarious!" Then she looks at Carlos and her eyes bug out. "What? You're standing!"

Carlos walks around in a circle. "And now I'm walking! Man, this is a CRAZY DAY!"

Zoe looks down at her phone and frowns. "Uh-oh, it's fading to glitter, but here's one more post from Loopy!" She hands it over so I can see just before it disappears. It's a picture of a sign, and it says "26 steps to the Pedestal!"

"Come on! He's almost here!" My friends and I run out of the golden elevator and outside to the pedestal of the Statue of Liberty.

We're met by a concrete barrier, which is helpful because it keeps us from falling down to the bottom of the Statue of Liberty. I stare out over the water, toward the New

York City skyline. The cold breeze whips right through me and sends a chill all the way down to my toes.

"Whoa. That's DOPE!" It's the opposite view from when I was on top of the Empire State Building. The Statue of Liberty looked so small from over there. But from here . . .

I throw my head back and stare up at the turquoise statue. I can see her left elbow and the book she's holding.

Even the Statue of Liberty reads.

"This thing is huge!" Scratchy is also leaning back, looking at the statue. "You think we could go up there? To the crown?"

"Probably. I mean, Carlos is walking, so I'm thinking we can do pretty much anything we want right now. But we gotta find Loopy first!"

A security person with a smile on her face comes over to greet us. "Hey, kids, are you enjoying the view?" She points to my shorts. "Aren't you cold?" Then she laughs. "Never mind. I'm sure you're not. Little kids are never cold." She takes a look left, then right. "Have you lost your parents? Or are you on a school field trip?"

I reach into my shorts pocket and pull out a picture of Loopy. "Actually, we're looking for my dog. We think he came up here. Can you help us find him?"

I show her the picture. She gives me a funny look. "Your *dog*? Honey, no dogs are allowed up here." But then her eyes get big when she looks a little closer. "Hey, I know that dog!"

"You do? Is he *here*?" Zoe, Scratchy, and Carlos crowd around me.

She frowns. "No, like I said. Dogs aren't allowed. But

this dog . . . this little guy managed to ride the ferry over *and* he snuck up here one day. We tried to catch him but he was too quick! He was wearing a little camera or something on his head."

"Yes! That's HIM! That's Loopy! What day was that?"

She crunched her eyebrows together. "Oh, that was about three years ago! It happened the first week I was working here. Weirdest thing ever. I'll never forget it. We searched the whole island and alerted the ferry boat drivers, but no one ever spotted him again."

"THREE YEARS AGO?"

Zoe put her hand on my shoulder and pulled me back a step. The security girl put her hand on her hip. "Are you okay?" Then she looked around. "Who did you say you were here with?"

"He's fine." Zoe chuckles. "We know dogs aren't allowed. He's putting together a story for his English class about a dog who visits the Statue of Liberty. My brother gets carried away sometimes." Zoe tilts her head and rolls her eyes.

The woman nods. "Oh, okay. Well, hey, if it helps your story any, our security cameras got pictures of that dog up in the crown! That would be fun to put in a story. Do you have crown tickets?"

Zoe pulls something out of her backpack and hands it to the woman. "Are these crown tickets?"

The woman looks at the stack of papers and smiles. "Why yes, they are! Let me show you the way to the staircase. You'll have to leave your backpacks here, though. Only people and cameras are allowed."

"I never thought I'd be climbing stairs again!" Carlos grins ear-to-ear as he leads us up the metal spiral staircase toward the crown.

I huff and puff. "Carlos, slow down, man! We're dying back here!" I keep an eye out, above and below, for Loopy.

Zoe grabs me by the shoulder. "Arcade, don't get your hopes up. The woman said he was here three years ago."

I reach for my golden chain. "I know, but we have the power of pure gold working in our favor. And Carlos is walking! Anything can happen. I bet he's up here. I asked the token, remember?"

We keep climbing, and Zoe keeps talking. "You asked the token to bring you to the Statue of Liberty."

"I know. Because Loopy's here. Zoe, we HAVE to find him!"

"One hundred forty-six more stairs left!" Carlos calls out, his triumphant voice echoing off the walls of the pedestal. "This is the BEST DAY OF MY LIFE!"

Scratchy wipes sweat from his brow. "I'm glad YOU'RE enjoying it. This climb is making me itchy!"

I tune my ears for any sound of a Loopy bark, but all I hear are people, huffing and puffing. Finally, after a few more circles around the staircase, we come to a cramped area with little look-out windows.

"We're here! The crown!" Carlos bends down to touch his toes and stretch. Then he leans with both hands against a window to look out. A tear rolls down his cheek. Then he turns to me. "I don't know how you made this happen, Arcade, but thank you. Thank you SO much." Then he goes back to gazing out the window.

The crown is cramped and stuffy. Each of us stands next to a little window and stares out. The waves gently roll in toward the shore way down below. We are higher than everyone else on Liberty Island. They all look like ants from up here.

One of those ants could be Loopy.

"Aww, I miss the little Arcade." Zoe reaches over and messes my hair up with her hand. "You were so cute three years ago."

"*Three years*, Zoe. The token is late by three years. Why would it do that to me?"

Zoe looks me straight in the eyes, and then she points to Carlos. "Maybe this isn't about *you*."

Yeah, Arcade. Don't be so self-absorbed.

I walk over and stand next to Carlos.

He just keeps staring out at the city. "Man, I LOVE New York." He looks over at me. "And I LOVE THIS DAY."

And just as soon as he says that, something heavy drops on my chest, and golden glitter shoots out of the Statue of Liberty's torch.

"RADICAL!" Scratchy yells. "This is better than the 4th of July!"

The glitter plasters itself on all the windows, and two of the panes grow and stretch to become elevator doors. The golden coin slot pops up, right in the middle of them.

"Does this mean we have to go back home?" Carlos reaches down and rubs the tops of both his legs.

I hate to say it. "Yes. I'm sorry. Back to Dooley. And the test."

But maybe, just maybe, I passed this one.

Our backpacks are waiting for us in the elevator. And so is Carlos's wheelchair.

"Did we travel back in time?" Carlos asks as he marches in place, enjoying the last bit of wheelchair-free time. "Is that why I can walk? Is that why we all look so young?"

I take a look at my short arms and small feet. "I guess that's what's happening. I never know with this token. I wonder exactly how far back we went?"

Zoe is fishing in her backpack for something. She pulls out some small rumpled papers. "Here, this will tell us. The date is on our tickets." We crowd around to take a closer look. "See, today's date, October 26th, is stamped on the ticket. But the year is exactly three years ago!"

Scratchy starts counting on his fingers. "Arcade, if the security lady was right about seeing Loopy three years ago—"

Zoe interrupts. "And if we were just at the Statue of Liberty *three years ago*—"

I conclude, "Then we lost Loopy six years ago?"

Zoe smiles. "And we know we lost him in one of two places on Picture Post . . ."

I catch my breath. "And it couldn't have been at the

school, when Wiley was in third grade, because the math doesn't work out."

"So we had to have lost him when Wiley was riding his bike! On that street where the kids were making fun of him. When he broke Reagan's window!" Zoe grabs me by the shoulders. "And that makes sense, because that would have made Wiley . . ."

"A first grader! You guys, we've got to get to school and find out where Reagan Cooper lived in first grade!"

CHAPTER 31

Cheater, Cheater

HOPE YOU ARE ALL RESTED AND READY TO BE TESTED! HA! WE'RE GETTING IT OVER WITH, FIRST THING!" Mr. Dooley grinned as he passed out the math tests. This time Amber Lin passed out the scan sheets.

She placed a scan sheet on my desk. "Good luck, Arcade. This was a hard chapter."

"You're telling me." I glanced over at Wiley Overton just as he reached into his huge brown backpack and pulled out a paper, which he slipped under his test.

There's space on the test to show our work. No one needs that much scratch paper.

Yet, everyone in the room seemed to have it. All except Scratchy, Amber, Bailey, Carlos, . . . and me.

I pulled a number two pencil out of my backpack and checked to make sure the point was sharp. When I looked up, the door to our classroom was flung open. In walked our principal, Mr. Francis, with Reagan Cooper. She had her arms crossed, and she was smirking at . . .

Wiley Overton.

"HELLO, MR. FRANCIS."

"Hello, Mr. Dooley. I'm sorry to interrupt. Can I speak to you for one moment, please?"

Dooley got up from his desk and went out in the hallway with Reagan and Mr. Francis. When they came back in, Reagan was gone. Both men were staring at me.

"Arcade?" Mr. Dooley said. "Please put down your pencil and come out to the hallway."

I nodded. "Yes, sir."

"And Wiley? We'd like to see you too." Wiley got up.

"And bring your backpack, Mr. Overton," Mr. Francis said.

Yes! Maybe I'm gonna get my flamingos back!

Mr. Francis stood with his arms crossed. His big mustache looked like it had just been oiled and styled at a beauty salon.

Mr. Dooley spoke at a normal pitch. "Wiley, it's come to our attention that for the last few weeks, tests have been taken from my desk drawer, photocopied, and passed around, enabling many students on this campus to cheat on my tests. Are you in possession of any of those photocopies right now?"

Wiley put his backpack down on the floor and cracked his knuckles. He looked left, right, anywhere except at Mr. Dooley.

"Mr. Overton," Principal Francis said, "let me assure you, there *will* be consequences for cheating, but if you withhold any information that we find out about later, the consequences will be greater."

"Uh," Wiley cleared his throat, "yes, sir."

Mr. Francis uncrossed his arms. "I know you struggle with tests, so the temptation to cheat is great."

Wiley nodded.

"Do you have the test with you now, Wiley?" Mr. Dooley put one hand on his hip and rubbed his chin with the other.

Wiley looked down at the floor. "Yes, sir."

What am I doing here? I have nothing to do with this.

Mr. Francis put out his hand. "Let's have it then."

Wiley glanced over at me for a split-second, and then reached into his backpack and lifted out another backpack. It was black, with flamingos. No surprise there. He handed it to Mr. Francis. "Kids have been passing this around school every week. The tests and the answers are in it. I've been having trouble understanding math, so I've been using it to help me study. It's easier when I know what the questions are going to be. But I never look at them when I'm taking the test."

Mr. Francis unzipped the flamingo backpack and pulled out a folder filled with papers. He handed the stack to Mr. Dooley, who flipped through them. "My tests from the last few weeks," Dooley said, shaking his head.

"Unbelievable," sighed Mr. Francis, a concerned look on his face. Then he looked up at Wiley. "Where did this backpack come from? Who's the ringleader?"

Wiley shrugged. "I don't know, sir. After I'm done with it, I pass it to another kid. Then it makes the rounds. All I know is whose name is on the tag."

My stomach churned. My mouth ran dry. My fingers turned cold.

Mr. Francis picked up the backpack, pulled the tag up, and read, "Arcade Livingston." He glared at me. "This is your backpack?"

Mr. Dooley gave me a knowing, but confused glance.

He knows it's mine. He saw it last year, every day for those last six weeks when I attended PS 23. He often commented on it.

"Yes, sir," I said. "But I'm not the ringleader. I don't cheat. I lost that backpa—"

"Arcade," Mr. Francis's face was as serious as could be, "go gather your things and come with me to the office."

CHAPTER 32

Suspended!

Since Wiley was caught with the cheating materials, he got a zero on the test, with no chance of making it up.

Since I was implicated as the "cheating ringleader," I got a three-day suspension.

I lay on my bed that afternoon, staring at the ceiling.

"I wish I could live on the moon," I said to the empty room, "away from every other living soul." The Triple T Token gave a sizzling jolt against my chest. I cupped the pure gold in my palm. "No, not now. I can't run away from my trials. But do you still believe I'm the right kid for the job? What kind of reputation must I have?"

There was a knock at the door.

"Go away, Zoe."

The door opened. It was my mom and dad. I dropped the token inside my shirt and I sat up.

"Who were you talking to, bud?" Dad came over and sat at the foot of my bed.

"Well, let's see, it couldn't have been my dog, because he's lost. And it couldn't be my best friend, because . . .

well . . . he's lost too. I guess I was just talking to the air. That's all I have left."

Mom smiled a little and sat down on the edge of my bed. "Well, I heard what you said about your reputation, and I'd like to respond to the question, if you don't mind."

I ran my hand through my hair. "Fine with me."

"Your father and I *both* believe you are not a cheater. We are anxiously waiting for all the facts to come in and hope you will be proven innocent as soon as your principal interviews a few of the students. Take heart, Arcade. Your reputation hasn't changed with the people who love you the most."

I started to cry a little. "But Wiley *lied* about me! He stole my backpack in the subway and used it to pass the tests around. I saw him break the lock on Mr. Dooley's desk. *He's* the ringleader! How could he do that to me? I've been nothing but nice to him!"

My stomach churned. I remembered the poster of Wiley that I brought back from Picture Post, the one that read: WHINY OVERTON–DUMBEST KID IN THIRD GRADE.

I should use that to get revenge against Wiley. That would show him! I can't believe I ever felt sorry for him.

As soon as I thought that, the token shot heat through my body.

"Owww!"

Dad walked over and put his hand on my shoulder. "Arcade, I know it hurts. People can behave badly, and that sometimes causes innocent people to suffer. But we don't have to let what they do stick to us. We ask God to help us rise above it, forgive them, then we keep living the way we know is right. If you do that with Wiley, he'll see that you're different from others. And then *he* may turn around! Remember, let kindness and loyalty never leave you."

I nodded. "Tie them around your neck as a reminder."

Dad smiled. "Then you will find favor with both God and people, and you will earn a good reputation. Exactly. Arcade, I think you're the right kid to do just that."

The token jumped inside my shirt.

"And I'm sorry about all your losses lately," Mom said. "I lost something very valuable once."

Butterflies flew around in my stomach. "What did you lose?"

"A piece of jewelry. I know, it's not as big a deal as a dog or a friend, but it was really special, because your father gave it to me when we were dating."

She stopped talking. I looked at her. "So, what happened?"

Mom folded her hands in her lap. "I was really upset. For quite a long time."

"That's not very encouraging, Mom."

She laughed softly. "I'm sorry. I did get over it, finally."

"How?"

She looked Dad in the eyes. "I focused on everything I *hadn't* lost. And I learned to be grateful for those things. Plus, I figured that whoever ended up with that piece of jewelry needed it more than I did."

"I'm not sure anyone needs Doug or Loopy more than me."

Mom reached over and hugged my neck. "I agree. And that's why I'm praying that we get them both back very soon."

Later that night, I thought about what Mom said.

She's praying we get them *both* back?

Are she and Dad considering adopting Doug? That would be awesome! But they have no idea that Loopy is lost in Picture Post.

That reminded me of something important! I was supposed to talk to Reagan Cooper today, but that whole cheating fiasco got me off track. I grabbed my phone and typed up a text.

Hi Coop. I'm not a cheater.

I clicked send.

She responded immediately.

I know. I'm sorry you got in trouble for it. Rotten Whiny Overton!

I texted back.

I have a question.

She responded.

Shoot.

Do you remember what street you lived on
when you were in first grade?

Yeah. That's easy.

WHERE?

I waited for a response. For an hour! Did her phone die?
Was she teasing me? WHAT WAS GOING ON?

Then it came through. An emoji, the one with the
tongue hanging out, and a message.

*Sorry. Mom took the phone till I finished
homework. When I was in first grade, I
lived in the same place I do now!*

Really? Where is that?

West 77th.

My stomach felt like it jumped into my throat. Just nine
blocks south of me!

*Hang on, Loopy! I'm coming to find you! Just as soon as I can
get this token to heat up!*

For the next two weeks, I rubbed the token, I talked to the token, I spun it around on the chain, I pounded it into my chest. But nothing happened.

One Saturday morning, I lost it. "Heat up, you ROTTEN chunk of gold!" I immediately apologized. "I'm sorry, I didn't mean it. I know you're testing me, and I HATE it! Okay, maybe I understand a little. But it sure seems like you're picking on me! Can't you give a guy a break? It's almost the holidays and I could use a little Christmas cheer!"

Zoe pounded on my door. "ARCADE! OPEN UP!" She busted in. "We have another Loopy post! And your silly dog now has 1,000 followers!" Zoe handed me the phone.

"What is this picture?" I asked. "Looks like a building under construction."

"Yeah, that's what it LOOKS like. You need to enlarge it. You won't believe it!"

I pressed my thumb and forefinger to the screen and pulled them apart. The picture zoomed in. The construction was tall, with pieces of wood layered on different levels of that famous

New York City scaffolding. In between the wood pieces, looked like . . . tree branches?

"It's the Rockefeller Center Christmas tree, Arcade! They're decorating it! And Loopy's there!"

As soon as she said that, the token began to burn.

I handed Zoe her phone back, pulled out the token, and rubbed it between my palms. "Today's the day, Zoe! I know how far back in time to go now."

Gold, red, and orange glitter swirled around my room, like autumn leaves falling from the Central Park trees.

"Be careful, Arcade! I can't believe I'm saying this, but remember what Doug said—*Be specific!*"

"Well, I know we can't go back six years in age. I was a doofus in first grade."

"You're a doofus now."

"Very funny. But a first grader can't run around New York City alone. So, I have to be specific about that. I know what to say."

My closet doors turned to golden doors, and I held the token in my hands, close to my heart.

"Take us to Rockefeller Center six years ago. But keep us the age we are now."

I looked over at Zoe, and she smiled and nodded. Was she actually excited to go on an Arcade adventure?

The golden coin slot popped up, looking like a miniature doghouse.

"Throw it in, Arcade!"

I did. It fell with a clunk through the top of the roof. I clapped my hands together and then pulled them apart. The doors opened.

Christmas carols play over the elevator speakers.

> Oh, Christmas tree, oh, Christmas tree,
> How lovely are your branches . . .

I hum along. "That's nice. Christmas music always makes me feel hopeful." I breathe in deep and imagine how much slobber will be on my face if I can just find Loopy.

The ride is short, and the elevator doors open up onto an ice-skating rink.

"So where's our skates?" Zoe looks around the elevator. "You didn't ask for skates?"

Zoe shoves me out and, on the first step, I slip, slide, and spin around on my backside. When I finally stop, I look up. "HEY! There's the tree!"

Zoe steps out but doesn't slide. She just turns around in those black boots of hers that have killer gripper-treads on the bottom. She looks up at the tree. "Nice. But we can't go up there without getting stopped by security. How are we going to find Loopy?"

I put my fingers to my mouth and I whistle. I'm not a great whistler, though. It always sounds like a dying squirrel or something. But Loopy knows the sound.

We both stand there on the ice, looking up at the massive tree, while skaters whizz by. Workers are installing lights on all levels of the Rockefeller Christmas tree.

"If he's up there, he'll come out. I'm the only one in the world who whistles like that."

"And that's a very good thing," Zoe says.

We wait and we watch. I whistle again.

Zoe puts her fingers in her ears. "Come out, Loopy, and save my eardrums."

And then we see him! On the tallest level, of course!

"Loopy! Come down here, boy!" I yell at the top of my lungs.

Woof! Woof!

He turns and runs toward the middle of the tree. I can't see him anymore.

"Come on, Zoe! We have to get to the base of the tree, ASAP!"

I grab Zoe's hand and we run off the ice. Well, at least Zoe does. I just slip again and slide head first like a baseball player into home plate. I do this several times till we reach the exit.

"Arcade! This way!" Zoe waves her arms and runs around the ice rink, up toward the monster-tree construction site.

How many lights do they use on this thing, anyway? Over 50,000. You read it in New York City: A Coffee Table Tour.

I'm finally able to pull myself off the ice and make some tracks. I run as fast as a person can when weaving through New York City crowds. Most of the people are taking pictures of the tree and *not* trying to move out of my way. I whistle again, but it's drowned out by the sounds of honking horns, construction vehicles, and workers hammering up in the tree.

We finally reach the base. Well, as close as we can get. A short barrier keeps us from it.

"Excuse me, sir? Can I come in there? My dog is on the top level of the tree."

The security guard looks at me and laughs. "A dog? There are no dogs up there. Just construction elves."

"Are you sure?" Zoe says. "He's a little shih-poo, and he's wearing a head camera."

"A head camera?"

"Yeah! And he's taking pictures for his Picture Post account." Zoe tries to show him on her phone but it's all glittery. "Sorry. My phone is broken."

The security guard looks confused, but he pulls out his phone. "I've got Picture Post. What's his username?"

I take a deep breath. "@LoopDogNYC."

The man pokes letters on the phone, and then grabs his head. "What?!?" He turns the phone so I can see it. Loopy's posted a picture from the top of the tree, looking down at the ice. There's a kid sprawled out on his stomach.

I laugh. "Yes! That's me!"

The security guard hollers up to the workers in the tree. "HEY, GUYS! You got a little dog up there anywhere?"

One of them calls down. "We did but he booked it outta here! He ran off that way, toward the ice rink!"

I look, and there he is. In the middle of the ice. Looking back at me!

Woof! Woof!

"LOOOOOOOPY! STAAAAAAAY!"

Loopy takes off.

"Now you did it, Arcade," Zoe says. "Loopy never stays."

"Oh, yeah! I forgot! Come on!"

We run back down toward the ice. "Have you seen a little dog?" We ask people in the crowd as we run by.

"Yes!" An older woman standing near the railing points her thumb away from us. "He went that way, toward Times Square. He had a little camera on is head. He was so cute. But you better hurry! He's quick!"

CHAPTER 34

Not Fair, Times Square

e's gonna get squashed in all that traffic!" I grab Zoe's hand and we huff and puff across 50th Street, turning south on 7th, toward Times Square. We run right into a huge crowd, holding up signs and yelling. NYPD officers stand around the crowd, watching carefully.

"Oh, no! It's a protest!" Zoe stops and tries to catch her breath.

"A protest? That's dope! I wonder what they're protesting?"

"We can Google protests from six years ago later. Right now, we need to figure out a way to get through."

I grab Zoe's sleeve. "Come on, we'll go around!" We run back to 50th, and this time we cut south on—you guessed it—Broadway.

"Ugh! I'm NOT a fan of Broadway!" Zoe yells as we weave around the tourists who are gawking up at all the theater signs.

Then I spot something. "HEY! There's Dad's show!"

We stop for a moment to look. It's hard to tell if it's a large or small theater by the front of it. The marquee is cool.

Old-fashioned style, with lights all around the elevator-door shaped sign. And in the middle, in rounded letters, it says:

MANHATTAN DOORS—A MUSICAL

I smile. "I'm proud of you, Dad." A lump forms in my chest. No, wait . . . something lumpy has fallen on my chest! *Uh-oh.*

***

Glitter rains down. I try to wave it away. "NOOOOOO! I haven't found Loopy yet!" Golden elevator doors appear on the sidewalk, right there in the middle of bustling New York tourists, who walk right through them on their way to their many destinations.

A golden coin slot juts out from the center of the doors. Zoe stands close to me. "I don't see Loopy anywhere." She stares at the doors. "I don't suppose we can stall, can we?"

I shake my head. "The one time I tried to stall, I almost didn't make it back." I look down and pull the token off my chain. "The lady said that I'm supposed to trust the tester. But with each disappointment, it's getting harder and harder to do that." The token snaps and sparks. And now, so does the coin slot.

Zoe pats me on the shoulder. "Go ahead, throw it in." She tilts her head toward the coin slot. "We'll find him. Maybe not this time, but soon."

I look around one last time, just in case the little furball is somewhere close by. Nope. I flip the coin up and watch it tumble into the slot. The doors open, and I stifle a sob as we enter.

Not fair, Times Square. You have my dog.

CHAPTER 35

Golden Plans

After we returned, Zoe and I sat quietly on the front steps of our brownstone, trying to figure out our next move.

"So let's review," Zoe said. "You can control the token, but not till it heats up, right?"

I inhale and exhale deeply. "Seems like it."

"And you've been specific each time with your requests."

"I have, but Loopy's still lost. Do you think the token is punishing me for something?"

"Punishing you? That's ridiculous! What do you need to be punished for? You haven't done anything wrong. You're one of the most caring and helpful people I know."

I glanced over at my sister. "Would you mind recording that so I can play it back whenever you need to be reminded of it?"

She pushed me in the arm. "Record what? I didn't say a thing." She laughed under her breath.

I laughed along with her. But then a thought hit me. There were a couple of people who I *could* help that I had been ignoring.

The Badgers. They asked me to redeem them.

I bolted to my feet. "Zoe! I think I know what I need to do!"

She stood up next to me. "What?"

"I need to bring the Badger brothers back."

"Oh, no. No, no, no, Arcade! The Badger brothers don't deserve to be saved after all they've done!"

"But don't you see? I've been acting just like them. I've been greedy and sneaky and . . . what did you call me? Self-absorbed! Why should I expect the power of the token to help *me*, if I withhold its power to help *them*?"

Zoe plopped back down and buried her face in her hands. "Arcade, I hate this! If you bring them back here, who knows what they'll do! They want your token, and they'll stop at nothing to take it away from you."

"So? What if I just give it to them? They'd leave me alone then, right?"

"But they'd abuse the power."

I shrug. "And that would only hurt them. As for me, I'd just go back to being the ultra-cool person I always was."

"Without Loopy and Doug. And then you wouldn't have the token to help you get them back."

"And Flames will never make it back to the Beijing Zoo."

"Well, you could always get on a plane to China and deliver him yourself. You don't need the token for that. Sure, it would take a while. You'd have to save for the plane ticket, convince Mom and Dad—"

"THAT'S IT, ZOE!"

"What's it?"

"You just gave me an idea of how to bring the Badgers back but keep them away from me for a while."

"How?"

I stood up and walked down the stairs. "I'll tell you while we go feed Flames. I just have to make sure I'm super specific when the time comes!"

"We're getting low on shrimp again." I dumped a bunch in a bowl in Doug's kitchen, and then Zoe and I made our way up the stairs to the extra bathroom. Zoe pinched her nose as we walked in the door.

"Hey, Flamesy! Great to see you, bud! Want some shrimp?"

Flames flapped his feathers and glided over to me.

SQUAWK!

"Zoe, look how *orange* he is!" I elbowed her in the side.

"He's getting big. We can't leave him in here much longer."

"I know. He needs some sunshine too. You think we could take him out to the Ramble?"

"The RAMBLE? How would we do that?"

"Don't know. Maybe transport him in Milo's old cage that's in the storage room. We could cover him with a blanket on the way over, and then find a secluded spot to let him out for a bit."

Zoe paced around the little bathroom. "That's a nutty idea. I want nothing to do with it."

"But your goal is to watch birds in the Ramble. Don't you want to work on your goal?"

My phone rang. It was Doug requesting a face chat.

I put down the shrimp, and Flames began to devour it. Then I clicked *accept*.

"Hey, Doug! How's it goin', bro?"

Doug was wearing a floppy sun hat. "It's goin' awful, Arcade. It doesn't feel like Thanksgiving is just a week away. It's hot here, and I'm getting a suntan. It's weird. What are you doing?"

I flipped the screen to show him our flamingo friend. "We're feeding Flames, who is going through shrimp like there's no tomorrow. Thankfully, Mr. Dooley's brother keeps sending care packages. I think he must suspect something."

"That's AWESOME! How's Gram's house? Besides the smell?"

I could see the pain in Doug's eyes.

"It's good, Doug. Nice, as always. I just wish you were here."

Doug sighed. "Me too. But hey. I'll be there next week. It's my birthday the day before Thanksgiving, and the care facility is going to make an exception and let me stay with Gram for a few days. We have another appointment with the social worker about something."

"THAT'S DOPE! We gonna hang out, right?"

"We gonna hang out, right?"

"That's what I said."

"Yep, that's what you said." Doug laughed.

"Something's goin' down soon, Zoe, I can feel it!" I was jittery as we dug through the storage room to find Milo's old cage for Flames. I had to sit down on an old stool to stop my hands from shaking.

"I can't believe Mom keeps some of this old junk of ours." Zoe pulled out a photo album from a dusty box and flipped through it. "Huh. This is interesting. People actually printed out photos back in the day."

I stood up and walked over to look.

"Hey, check this out." Zoe pulled a white book out of the box and opened it. "Here's Mom and Dad's wedding pictures. They look like little kids!"

Zoe pointed to a really nice picture of Mom and Dad coming back down the aisle after their wedding ceremony. "They're positively glowing! Look at them!"

I took the book from her. "Oh, brother. Quit being so mushy, Zoe."

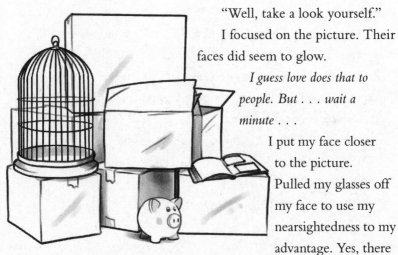

"Well, take a look yourself."

I focused on the picture. Their faces did seem to glow.

I guess love does that to people. But . . . wait a minute . . .

I put my face closer to the picture. Pulled my glasses off my face to use my nearsightedness to my advantage. Yes, there was something else glowing. Mom wore a golden chain, and whatever hung on that chain was glowing right through her high-necked dress.

The token around my neck sparked and jumped and sent a jolt of heat to my head. I grabbed the chain and pulled the token out from under my shirt. "Oh, man, here we go!"

Zoe dropped the book. "You've got flames coming out of that thing, Arcade! It's going to burn you!"

I held it out as far as I could. "It's never been this hot before, Zoe! What do I do?!?"

Do I ask for Doug, Loopy, or . . . help for the Badgers?

I licked my fingers and tried to touch the token. "It's too hot! How am I supposed to get it off the chain?"

Gold glitter swirled inside the storage room. It flew up my nose, in my mouth, and coated my eyelashes. Zoe began throwing boxes around, frantically searching for something. Finally, she handed me an old baseball glove from when I played T-ball. "Here! Pull it off with this!"

I shoved the glove on one hand while holding the chain out with the other. As Zoe reached over to help me, Milo's cage enlarged and turned into elegant elevator doors with shapes of flamingos etched in them.

"Now pull the token off with your glove and BE SPECIFIC with your request."

I reached up with the puffy leather fingers and, after a few fumbles, was able to pinch the token. It came off the chain, as usual, and it dropped in the netted pocket of my glove. Immediately, it started to burn through the leather.

"Get rid of it, Arcade! Throw it in the coin slot!"

"But Zoe, I can't *see* a coin slot!" This had never happened before. There *had* to be a coin slot, right?

Trust the tester . . .

"Take us back to San Francisco!" I yelled. "To the year 1937. To the Badger brothers. I want to help bring them home!" Then, right as the token was about to burn a hole through the glove, I flipped it up in the air. It sparked and flamed. The words on the back—Arcade Adventures— glowed brighter than ever as the token fell.

My old piggy bank sitting on the floor of the storage room turned gold and pulsed light. The token fell in the slot at the top.

Here we go . . .

I slapped my hands together, pulled them apart, and the doors opened.

CHAPTER 36

Badgering the Badgers

The elevator is full of fog.

Let me guess . . . San Francisco?

Last time we were here, the doors opened up on top of the unfinished Golden Gate Bridge. This time, I was hoping to arrive a couple of years later, but where?

Zoe drums her fingers on the side of the elevator. "I'm scared, Arcade. What if they're staring us right in the face when the doors open?"

"I never thought of that, Zoe. Thanks. Now I'm scared."

"You're welcome."

"It must be a pain living in your brain."

The fog increases and the temperature drops inside the elevator.

"I think maybe I've changed my mind about giving them the token." I reach for my empty chain. It's ice cold.

"Good."

"So does that mean you'll fight them with me?"

"Always."

"Thanks."

Why aren't the doors opening?

Now the fog is so thick I can't see anything.

"Zoe?"

"Yes?"

"Stay close, okay?"

She grabs my hand. "I got your back."

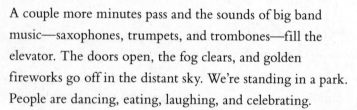

A couple more minutes pass and the sounds of big band music—saxophones, trumpets, and trombones—fill the elevator. The doors open, the fog clears, and golden fireworks go off in the distant sky. We're standing in a park. People are dancing, eating, laughing, and celebrating.

Okay, this isn't so bad.

Everyone is dressed up, and I wonder if I'll recognize the Badger brothers if I actually do see them. Someone taps me on the shoulder. I freeze.

"Arcade?"

It's a woman's voice, but it's not Zoe. Zoe's still standing next to me with a terror grip on my hand. She looks like she's going to faint. I shake her hand off and turn around.

I breathe a small sigh of relief. "Oh. It's you." I nudge my sister. "Zoe, meet . . . uh . . . the Triple T woman."

Zoe's mouth drops open. The woman standing in front of both of us is the lady who I keep seeing and who Zoe never sees. She's wearing her usual white sweat suit and the ball cap with the three glowing Ts on it.

"Hello, Zoe," the woman says. "You are a loyal sister to Arcade."

Zoe can't say a word.

The woman continues, "I know, you don't always see eye-to-eye. Little brothers can be a real pain. And, by the way, a stop sign *is* an octagon, with only eight sides." The woman grins at Zoe and then winks at me. "And in the grand scheme of things, does it really matter?"

I nod. "Yes, it does!"

She laughs. "I knew you would say that." Then she tips her head to the side. "You caught them on a good day. I think they'll be glad to see you. But I wouldn't trust them just yet. Stay with your plan."

"Okay," I say. "But what should I say to them?"

"You'll think of something." She turns and vanishes into the crowd.

"WAIT! I have questions!" Zoe yells, and she holds a hand out.

"Too late," I say. "She's a fast one."

* * *

I scan the crowd and see them. They're wearing old-fashioned suits and hats. They clean up well. They are holding drinks, talking with one another, and looking up at the Golden Gate Bridge. I take small steps toward them, and Zoe follows. We get close enough to eavesdrop.

"Feels good, doesn't it? To know we helped build that

thing?" One of the brothers gestures to the other, and then takes a sip of his drink.

"Yes. It reminds me of when we first went into business. We could do anything together. No stoppin' us."

"Makes me wish we'd never found that token," the first brother says. "I don't think it did us any favors."

"I agree. I wonder how that kid is getting along with it?"

It's now or never, Arcade.

"Excuse me, Mr. Badger?" I barely squeak the words out. The brothers turn around. Zoe grabs my hand and squeezes it tight.

"Hey! Look who it is! The kid came to our rescue after all. I told you he would, Lenwood!" Kenwood steps forward. "So how has it been with the token, Arcade? That's your name, right? Have you been traveling all over the world? How about the testing? Do you like being tested?"

"I hated that part," Lenwood says.

I try to change the subject. "You guys built a nice bridge. Sorry I left you hanging. I didn't know how to control the token back then." I swallow hard. "But I got your letter . . ."

Lenwood's eyes open wide. "You got our letter? Whoa. That was a long shot! Are you here to take us back?"

"Yes, I'm here to take you back to present day." I finger my golden chain. "That is, if the token comes back and it listens to me again. It's a little unpredictable."

Kenwood chuckles. "Oh, you don't have to tell us about that token. The thing made us crazy. But all is forgiven. Just like we wrote in the letter. We made up, and we're ready to move on."

"So, you've forgiven *each other*?" Zoe's words echo a little in the night air.

Lenwood glances over at Kenwood. "Yeah. We're working *together* now."

Stay with your plan, Arcade.

Our conversation is interrupted by a large round of fireworks—the grand finale. Bursts of gold, red, and orange light up the sky, with the Golden Gate Bridge in the background.

"They've been having parties in this park all week to celebrate the opening of the bridge," Lenwood says. "But today, we celebrate our return home!" He reaches out and puts his arm around Kenwood. "You think grandma will be happy to see us?" Lenwood turns to me. "Did you know Miss Gertrude is our grandma?"

"Yeah, she told me that once." The warning in her letter flashes in my mind:

> *Do not try to bring them back.*

The grand finale crackles and sparkles. The crowd oohs and aahs. As the last fireworks explode, I feel the token drop back on my chest. It pulses heat like a flaming heartbeat. Or maybe it's just my heart, beating out of my chest. Glitter falls from the fireworks in the sky and covers the grass in front of us. The last firework shoots out and draws an outline of elevator doors in the sky. They come and land in front of us. A golden coin slot, shaped like the Golden Gate Bridge, rises up from the ground. A little sign next to it says *Pay Toll Here*. I reach inside my shirt and, while Lenwood and Kenwood step toward the doors, I pull the token off the chain, put it between both my palms, and speak softly.

"Take the Badger brothers to present day San Francisco. Then take me and Zoe home."

"C'mon kid! Open the doors!"

I can see in the eyes of the brothers the same thing I saw on that fateful day I left them hanging on the bridge. Greed. I wonder if Miss Gertrude was right. They aren't ready yet.

Oh, well, here goes.

I step forward and deposit the token. Then I make the open-door motion with my hands. The doors open and the Badger brothers run in, laughing and yelling. "Finally! We're going home!" And then, to my surprise, the doors close right behind them!

"ARCADE!" Zoe freaks out. "What did you just do? WE MISSED THE ELEVATOR!"

I hold my palms to the sky. "I don't know what I just did!" But one thing I finally know for sure.

I trust the tester.

"We just need to wait for the next elevator, Zoe."

"The NEXT elevator?"

"Yeah. You live in New York City, right? There's always another elevator."

Sure enough, another elevator appears! But this time, there is no coin slot. That's fine, because I don't have the token anyway. When the doors open, the Triple T lady is standing inside, smiling. She steps out.

"Happy travels," she says, just like the first time I met her, in the Ivy Park Library. "You're about to have a delightful—and definitely not boring—Thanksgiving."

We step inside the elevator and she winks at me as the doors close.

CHAPTER 37
A Definitely Not Boring Thanksgiving

It's the coldest Thanksgiving in a century here in New York City!" The TV commentator shivered in her big, red puffy coat as she held the microphone. "And those balloons may not fly if this wind doesn't calm down."

Zoe, Doug, and I sat wrapped in blankets munching on cinnamon rolls and bacon. We were getting ready to watch the Macy's Thanksgiving Day Parade while Mom and Dad began the process of cooking turkey and all the other traditional stuff for our mid-afternoon feast.

"That's cool your gram let you stay over last night," I said to Doug.

"Yeah. A guy only turns twelve once in his life, and Gram thought I'd enjoy it more spending it with my best friend. I'll hang out with her tonight." Doug reached into a bag next to him and munched a corn chip. "Thanks for the birthday food bucket! I'll probably eat it all before I have to go back to . . . ugh . . . balmy Florida."

Zoe got up and looked out the frosty front window of

our brownstone. "I can't believe we went from the hottest summer to the coldest Thanksgiving ever!"

"I wonder how Elijah is doing with getting business in Central Park?"

"Probably not so well." Zoe shook her head. "But he'll find a way to enjoy the process, and he'll smile through the cold. You know, we should be out there, too, watching the parade live! It starts just a few blocks south from us. We could be there in twenty minutes."

I wrapped up in my blanket a little tighter. "BRRRRRRR."

"Yeah," Doug said. "BRRRRRRRRR!"

Zoe looked over at us and rolled her eyes. "Babies."

Zoe's phone buzzed. "Hello? Oh . . . hey, Michael . . . yes, I'm looking out the window right now . . . it's crazy cold . . . what? Um . . ."

Zoe hopped behind the love seat and sat down, where we couldn't see her. I jumped onto the love seat so I could hear what she was saying.

". . . Yes, that would be fun . . . but aren't you going with Trista? Broke up? . . . I'm sorry, Michael . . . yeah, I get it . . . Broadway strikes again . . . well, okay . . . that would be fun . . . let me ask my parents . . . yeah. . . . I have a warm coat . . ."

I popped my head over the love seat just as Zoe was standing, and we almost bumped heads.

"Arcade! Were you listening to my conversation?"

Before I got a chance to answer, Zoe's phone buzzed again. She looked down at her screen. "It's a notification from @LoopDogNYC!"

I pulled the phone from her hands to take a look. It was a new Picture Post of Loopy's furry, chocolate-colored legs, standing in front of a giant balloon being held to the ground under a net!

I ran upstairs. Doug followed. "What's goin' on, Arcade?'

I flew into my room and began piling on clothes. "Today's the day, Doug. We're gonna get Loopy back!"

"We're gonna get Loopy back?"

"That's what I said! He's over in the Thanksgiving parade balloon area!"

Zoe barged in my room. "But he's there six years ago! How is that going to help us get him back?"

I checked to make sure my token was still there under all my layers. "We just have to wait for the token to heat up, and I know *exactly* what to say when it does. But we have to be close to where Loopy is . . . I mean was . . . six years ago. So I guess it's balloon time, my good people!"

We finished throwing on all the warm clothes we could find, then told Mom and Dad that we wanted to be like real New York City residents and see the Macy's parade live.

"You want to go in *this* weather?" Mom reached for my scarf and pulled it tight.

"I think it's a great idea," Dad said. "It fits with your goal to experience New York City. And why not experience it in the bitter cold! Just make sure you all stay together so nobody gets lost."

"Will do, Dad!" I practically flew out the door. Doug and Zoe followed. Michael Tolley was waiting at the bottom of our brownstone steps.

"Oh, hey, Michael." Zoe pulled her pink beanie down over her ears. "I hope you don't mind if Doug and Arcade tag along. They want to see the parade too. Is that okay?"

Michael grinned. "Sure! Let's go. It will be interesting to see if any of the balloons fly away in this wind!"

When we reached the corner of Central Park West and 86th, we met up with Scratchy, Carlos, and Reagan Cooper.

"Happy Thanksgiving, friends!" Scratchy said. "Do you love the cold or what? I go from getting sunburned to windburned to frostbitten. Gotta love New York!"

"Zoe got a new Picture Post from @LoopDogNYC! He's over by the parade balloons!" In this mix of company, I couldn't mention that he's there six years ago.

"RADICAL!" Scratchy yelled. "Let's go get him. That would make this a great Thanksgiving."

"Who's Loopy?" Reagan asked.

"Who's Loopy?" Doug said.

"He's my dog, and he's been missing for about two months." I showed Reagan the picture of Loopy that I kept folded up in my pocket.

When she saw it, she got a huge grin on her face. "Hey! I had a dog just like him when I was little."

"You did? Really?"

"Well, I only had him for a short time. I found him out wandering on the street one day, with a silly camera on his head."

WHAT!?!

"I looked for the owners, but no luck. My parents let

me keep him. He was so fun. Slobbery though. And really crazy." Reagan laughed. "I should have named him Loopy."

Zoe stepped closer to Reagan. "What happened to that dog?"

Reagan sighed. "Well, like I said, he was a little crazy. I liked to put that camera on him and go for walks to see what videos and pictures we could get. He got away from me a couple of times, and was gone for a day or two, but he always came back. Until the day before Thanksgiving. I was going to take him for a walk that night with my parents to see the balloon inflation, but before I could get the leash on him, he took off. I never saw him again."

That's it! The reason she never saw him again is because I got him back! Today's the day!

"Brrrr! We gotta move." Scratchy pulled the hood of his coat up over his head. "Let's go watch some balloon action!"

We continued down Central Park West and ran into a huge crowd.

"We'll never get close to the balloons now with the parade about to start," Zoe whispered to me. "We need a better plan."

"Or another Picture Post," I said. "Come on, Loopy."

Zoe took her phone out of her coat pocket and held it in her gloved hand so she wouldn't miss any new notifications. Michael stayed by her side as we made our way through the crowds to find a good viewing place. Then, he grabbed her hand. "I know just the place. Come on, guys!"

We weaved and bobbed through many spectators. By the time we got to 66th, we were jammed in. No movement at all.

"Let me get in front of you," Carlos said. "Stay close behind me. I'm about to part the Red Sea!"

We scrunched in close. As Carlos wheeled forward, people moved out of the way. Several even smiled and waved. "Hey, Carlos! Nice to see ya! Happy Thanksgiving!"

"Dude, you got a lot of fans around here," I said.

Carlos nodded. "Yeah, I was a bit of a celebrity after my accident. Not the way anyone wants to become famous, but it is what it is."

We followed Carlos's path all the way down to Columbus Circle, where we met up with our pedicab friend, Elijah!

"Hello, friends! Happy Thanksgiving!"

"Hey, Elijah! Are you getting much business today?"

Elijah shook his head. "Today is not a working day for me. Today, I give thanks for all of God's blessings."

"Would you like to watch the parade with us?" I asked.

"I would love to."

Carlos managed to clear a path for us to stand, looking out toward Columbus Circle. Twenty minutes later, the parade began. Everyone else in the giant crowd had their eyes fixed upward, on the massive balloons, but mine scanned back and forth between Zoe's phone screen and the street—anywhere that a little fluffy dog might roam.

And then it happened. A huge gust of wind brought gasps from the crowd, and the kids holding the Pillsbury Doughboy balloon were pulled violently toward Columbus Circle. Red, orange, and yellow leaves fluttered down from the trees. As they dropped on our heads, they turned to glitter bombs.

The cold breeze cut through all my layers and turned me to ice. All except the area above my heart, which now produced a steady burn. I reached for Zoe.

"Anything on Picture Post?"

She checked. "Yeah. One just came in."

"THAT'S DOPE! Show me where he is!"

The token burned hot as I checked out Zoe's phone. It was a picture of Loopy, all right, and he was sitting in a sleigh, with Santa Claus!

Zoe put her gloved hand up to cover to her mouth. "Santa's at the end of the parade. We'll never get there through this crowd."

"We'll do the best we can. Hopefully the elevator will do the rest." I grabbed Doug by the elbow, and as the rest of the group was distracted by the Doughboy balloon, I pulled him toward the back of the crowd. Zoe followed.

"Hey! The SpongeBob balloon is coming! I don't wanna miss—"

"Doug, we have to go. The token is smokin'!" I dug through my scarf, coat, and two shirts to pull it out.

"The token is smokin'?"

"YES! That's what I said!"

"Okay, then, SpongeBob will have to wait."

I turned and ran back into Central Park, leaving most of the crowd behind.

Come on, doors, where are you? Santa's coming . . .

We ran north as fast as we could. Clouds formed in front of us and showered down gold glitter, leaving a trail to follow.

Come on, tester, you know the way.

We ran for a few more minutes, up over the Bow Bridge, to the sign that said we were entering the Ramble. The clouds dumped large flakes of glitter that solidified and formed doors, with a pulsing golden coin slot pushing out from the middle.

"Don't blow this, Arcade," Zoe said.

"Be specific," Doug clasped his hands like he was praying.

"Yeah," Zoe added. "Don't forget . . . six years ago . . . Thanksgiving . . . Santa Claus . . . and make us the same age as we are now."

I shook my head. "No. It's not as complicated as that, Zoe."

The token sparked and flamed and crackled. So did the coin slot.

"ARCADE! It *is* complicated! This is no time to get crazy with your thinking . . ."

I nodded and held the token between my burning gloves. "You're right. It's time to think . . . like Arcade Livingston."

I opened my hands and inspected the glowing Triple T Token. I smiled, flipped it up in the air, and said four words.

"Take me to Loopy."

"Ho, Ho, Ho!"

A man with a white beard wearing a red coat sits next to me on a sleigh, riding on a float above the crowd in New York City. And a little chocolate-colored shih-poo, wearing a head cam, sits on his lap licking his beard.

"LOOP! I FOUND YOU!"

Woof! Woof!

Loopy leaps onto my lap and snuggles up to my neck. His tail is wagging so hard it whips up and knocks my glasses crooked.

Oh, Loop.

Tears stream down my face while sweat seeps down my back.

Why is it so hot? The token isn't hanging around my neck right now.

"Wave to the crowd, Arcade." Zoe and Doug are sitting in front of me in the sleigh. They have peeled off their scarfs, coats, and mittens. It's a beautiful, sunny, not windy, and definitely-not-boring, Thanksgiving Day . . . six years ago.

"Hey, Santa!" Doug cranes his neck to talk to the jolly old guy. "You think you could give me a brother named Arcade for Christmas?"

Santa chuckles. "Ho, ho, ho! What kind of name is Arcade?" He gives me a little wink and a nod. "I'll work on it, but it sounds like you need a Manhattan Miracle."

As soon as he says that, white stuff begins to fall.

"What in the . . . it's too hot for snow," Zoe says, shaking her head.

"That's not snow, Zoe," I answer. "That's white glitter."

The doors delivered us back to the Ramble, and we had to apologize to our friends for the sneaky departure.

WE FOUND LOOPY, I texted to Scratchy.

RADICAL!!! he texted back. HAPPY THANKSGIVING, ARCADE.

"I hope Michael Tolley forgives you for ditching him again," I said, and I bumped Zoe as we walked through the Ramble paths back to 88th Street.

She grinned. "I have a feeling he will."

I put my finger inside my mouth and pretended to gag.

Zoe reached over to pet Loopy. "You crazy dog! Do you know that you have 2,500 followers on Picture Post?"

Loopy just stared at Zoe, unimpressed. Then he turned and sneezed in my face!

"Aw, COME ON, man! What are you doin'?"

He's just being Loopy. The best dog in the world.

★ ⬤ ★

My mom and dad were thrilled to see Loopy too. Mom ran to the door as soon as we came in. "Oh, you sweet little dog. We missed you so much. And what a great day to return!" She grabbed Loopy out of my arms and gave him a long snuggle.

"Food will be ready in an hour," Dad said. "How was the parade? Did you find a good viewing spot?"

Doug laughed. "Yeah, we pretty much got the best seat in the house."

Dad shot me a side glance. "Sounds interesting." Then he went over to the desk in the dining room and brought out a file. "While we have a minute, I'd like to talk to you kids about something."

Oh, no, now what? Will the testing never end?

Mom took Loopy over to the love seat and sat down. "We have a birthday present for you, Doug."

A birthday present?

That got my attention. I ran over and sat next to Mom.

Zoe threw all her cold weather clothes on the floor and plopped down on the couch. Doug just stood in the middle of the room. "Ah, you didn't have to get me another thing. That food bucket was the best!"

Dad sat down next to Zoe and opened the file. "Doug, we've been praying and planning and asking a lot of questions of your social worker . . ."

Doug narrowed his eyes. "My social worker?"

"And we went to visit your grandma," Mom added.

Doug smiled. "Really? Wow. I love my gram. I miss her a bunch."

"And she misses you." Dad stood up and walked toward Doug. "And, it's very interesting, but did you know that when you turn twelve, you have a little more say in where you want to live?"

Doug shrugged. "I do? I knew turning twelve was going to be cool."

Dad nodded. "Oh, it's cool all right. Anyway, we'd like to offer you a home here, with us."

"You'd like to offer me a home? Here? With you?"

"That's what I said, Doug."

Doug looked around. "For how long?"

"As long as you want. Now, I know we're not a perfect family—"

"Especially Arcade," Zoe said.

". . . but if you think you can stand us, we'd like to begin the adoption process."

Doug stood there, speechless. Actually, we all were. It was a moment I'll never forget.

Finally, Doug cracked a smile. "I'd love to live with you guys." Then he turned to me. "Dude, Santa works fast."

I don't think it was Santa, Doug. You just got a Manhattan Miracle.

CHAPTER 38

Bye, Bye, Flames

"Zoe! How's it look up there?"

"Ugh, this is SO embarrassing, Arcade!"

Flames munched shrimp while riding in Milo's cage, covered with a blanket. Doug and I pulled him in an old wagon we found in our storage room.

"We're going to get you outside for a little sunshine, my friend."

Zoe walked in front of us, scouting out empty paths in the Ramble. "I really don't know how you plan to keep him hidden from people."

"It's early on Black Friday, Zoe. Everyone's out shopping."

The Ramble was quiet. It seemed that even the birds were huddled up somewhere else.

"Can flamingos stand the cold?" Zoe shivered, and pulled the collar of her coat up.

"Yes! They can. According to my library book, *Feisty Flamingos,* as long as they have room to roam and lots of food, they can be happy in any climate."

"Yeah, well, we're running out of shrimp." Doug

scratched his head. "We're gonna have to get another donation from Dooley's brother pretty soon."

I pulled the blanket off the cage, opened the door, and helped Flames out. "Welcome to Central Park, Flames! You've been trapped in Doug's bathroom long enough."

Squawk! Squawk!

"Arcade, what if he flies away?" Zoe put her hand up to her mouth.

"Are you kiddin'?" Doug held out a large plastic bag of shrimp. "He won't leave the Food Dude."

Flames walked around on the dirt, just off the path in a little corner of the Ramble. Zoe and I sat on a bench, watching Doug follow Flames around.

"Well, here you go, sis. You're birdwatching in the Ramble. You can check off that goal." I licked my finger and then made a checkmark in the air. "You don't have to thank me."

"*Thank* you? I'm freaking out sitting here thinking that any minute we'll be arrested for sneaking a flamingo into a city park! Why would I thank you for *that*?"

I shook my head. "You're *so* dramatic."

"And you're so annoying . . ."

Doug snapped his fingers. "Hey! Bro! Sis! I won't tolerate this kind of bickering in my new family. Can't we just chill and hang with Mr. Flames here?"

Squawk!

At that moment, Flames began to flap his wings, and run. REAL FAST.

"Whoa! Wait up, Mister! That's not the way to the food!" Doug ran after Flames. Zoe and I got up and did the same.

"I told you this would happen!" Zoe huffed as she tried to keep up with Doug and me. Flames ran farther and farther into the Ramble.

"He's headed to the cave site!" Zoe yelled and pointed to a sign. "It's closed off! We can trap him there!"

Oh, yeah! The cave. That's DOPE!

Flames flew down a narrow Ramble path and under a metal rail post. Zoe, Doug, and I followed.

"Can flamingos navigate stairs?"

Flames disappeared down a stone staircase that lead deeper into the Ramble.

"Looks like the answer's yes," Doug said.

We flew down the stairs.

Zoe gasped. "The cave! There it is!"

It was blocked off to the public, *and* to flamingos, but I could see where people used to bring their boats in to hang out inside.

We had Flames cornered. Doug held out shrimp.

"How are we going to get him back to his cage now?" Zoe asked.

A hot sizzle shot through my torso. I reached down.

We're not done yet.

"I don't think he's going back to his cage. Or Doug's bathroom . . ."

The token didn't burn as hot as before. No flames, sparks, or snaps. When I pulled it out of my shirt, it glowed gold, and lights twinkled all around it.

"It's dazzling!" Zoe stared, mesmerized.

Glitter flew out of the token and transformed the boarded-up old Ramble cave into a beautifully carved, golden elevator. Gold flakes, *real* gold flakes by the looks of them, fell from the sky.

Doug gasped. "Where we gonna go, Arcade?"

Squawk!

I smiled at Doug. "What do you say we take Flames back to the Beijing Zoo?"

The elevator doors open right inside the bird house at the Beijing Zoo.

"Good job, Arcade," Zoe says with a little sass in her voice. "Being specific saves a lot of confusion."

The only problem is, I'm not ready to say goodbye.

"So this is where it all began," Doug says as he watches all the birds flying around. "I LOVE China!"

Zoe rolls her eyes. "Oh, brother. You need to see the giant pandas."

I reach down and smooth Flames's feathers. "I hope your family recognizes you now that you're orange."

"He's pink." Zoe laughs.

"Orange."

"Pink."

"Orange."

Squawk!

"Well," Zoe says. "Whatever color he is, he's home."

I look down at the ground. "I'm going to miss him. Taking care of him the last couple of months while searching for Loopy really kept me going."

"Well, we got a bathroom to renovate now. That'll keep the memories alive." Doug reaches over and pats me on the back as I reach down for one last flamingo hug.

"Take it easy, Flames. I hope they feed you top-notch shrimp here at the Beijing Zoo."

Flames wraps his neck around my arm and stays that way for a minute. Then he steps away, flaps his wings, and flies back into his *flamboyance* of flamingos.

"Let's go see the pandas while we still have time," Zoe says. She grabs Doug's elbow. I turn to follow, but then I spot someone off in the distance.

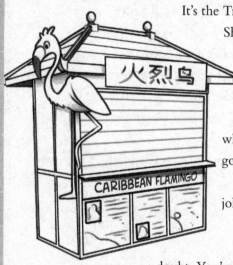

It's the Triple T woman.

She walks over to a kiosk next to the flamingo exhibit. I meet her there.

"You weren't joking when you said things were going to heat up."

She smiles. "I don't joke . . . about that."

"Did I pass the tests?"

She nods. "I had no doubt. You're compassionate and you wear loyalty and kindness . . ."

". . . around my neck as a reminder?" I finger my gold chain.

She looks me in the eyes. "There's so much more for you to learn, Arcade. And with each discovery, you can help someone be their best self."

"I like the sound of that. But I have some work to do. With the Badger brothers. And then there's Wiley Overton . . ."

"They'll come around. If they choose to."

The Triple T woman turns from me and points to the sign. "Flamingos are an odd bird. But I'm not surprised you like them. Do you know where the name flamingo comes from?"

I wrack my brain. In all my reading, I don't think I've ever come across that information.

I step toward the sign and read out loud what it says.

"The word 'flamingo' comes from the Spanish word 'flamenco,' which is derived from the Latin word 'flamma' meaning . . ."

WHAT???

"Flame. Or FIRE!"

"Dude! I've LITERALLY been surrounded by fire for the last three months! THIS IS DOPE!"

I turn, and the woman is gone.

"Zoe's never going to believe this!" I run toward the exit of the bird house. "Zoe! I have proof! Flamingos really ARE better than pandas!"

And right then, the Triple T Token—my little fiery metal tester—drops back on my chest.

Arcade and the Fiery Metal Tester Discussion Questions

1. Do you set goals for yourself? If so, what kinds of goals do you focus on? Goals of achievement, or goals to help you build your character? If you could pick a character trait to work on this year, what would it be?
2. If you were challenged to set a specific fun goal, what would it be?
3. Do you have places in your town that are famous tourist attractions, but you've never been to them? I challenge you to go to the library and find out about those places. See if you can visit them this year.
4. What is your favorite animal at the zoo? What do you think it would be like if you had a chance to have that animal as a pet? What adjustments would you have to make to your house? What foods would you have to keep around? If you don't know, do some research on that animal. Or better yet, visit the zoo and ask a zookeeper.
5. Have you ever had a good friend move away? How did you handle that difficult situation? Or were *you* the

friend who moved away? If so, how long did it take you to adjust to your new town? Was it easy or hard to keep in touch with your friends from your old town?

6. Do you think that going through trials can make you a better person? If so, how? What is a trial you have lived through? How do you think you are a better person because of it?

7. Had you ever heard the term "mettle" before reading *Arcade and the Fiery Metal Tester*? What situations in your life test your mettle? How are the words medal, metal, and mettle connected to each other in this book?

8. How did you feel about Wiley Overton when you first met him in this book? Did your feelings toward him change in the end? If so, what caused the change?

9. Do you have any friends with disabilities? If so, what have you learned from them about toughness and never giving up? What are some ways you can encourage them this week?

10. Have you ever failed a test? Did you fail because you didn't study, didn't pay attention, or because the subject matter was difficult to understand? How did you handle the failure? Did you do something different the next time that helped? What was it?

11. Are there people in your life who serve as mentors (experienced and trusted advisors)? If so, who are they? Do they seem peaceful to you? Can you ask them questions about life and share your frustrations with them? What kind of wisdom have they shared that has helped you?

12. Are you the kind of person who likes to control everything that happens? Do you think controlling *everything* is possible? How do you think trying to control things could hurt you or others?

13. If you were the owner of the Triple T Token (of course, that would be DOPE!), would you use it to help someone? Give an example of whom you might help and how.

14. The first T on the Triple T Token stands for TRAVEL. The second T stands for "TEST"? Did you figure that out? Why do you think it's important for people to go through tests in their lives in order for them to develop good character?

15. What do you think the third T stands for? Write your guess here: _____

16. While you are waiting for the 4th book in the Arcade series to come out, get some friends together to discuss the story so far. What do Arcade and his friends still need to learn about themselves and each other?

Acknowledgments

I owe an unpayable debt of gratitude to the only One through whom anything is possible for any of us. Thank you, Lord, for blessing me with the abilities and the guidance to live a life that far exceeds my childhood dreams. I pray that something we've done with this series thus far has made you proud.

Momma and Daddy Jennings—You are the headquarters for my heart. When I look back over my entire life, I can honestly say that I wouldn't change a thing about you. You stayed the course despite some of the most impossible odds and sacrificed more than I can fully imagine to make sure that I could go out into an uncertain world and succeed. I will always cherish everything about you both!

Jill Osborne—Who would have thought that after meeting just a year ago, we would be three amazing books in and working on an absolutely awesome fourth! I must tell you that I stand amazed at your creativity, dedication, and diligence. I don't know how long you work with authors on average, but something tells me that this series is just the beginning of years of outstanding work together on many incredible projects to come. Keep up the fantastic work! You are an extraordinary writer whom I am extremely proud to work with and know. Thank you! Thank you!!

Keith Bell—I still get a kick out of that .gif I sent you and Jill of Jim Carrey furiously typing at the keyboard in Bruce Almighty! I love it when you, Jill, and I get together to brainstorm for Arcade's adventures. I still don't know how you come up with so many amazing ideas and storylines. Best I can tell, you must be up in the wee hours of the morning going at the keyboard just like Bruce! Seriously though, I know that God has gifted you with a special level of creative thinking. And I truly appreciate all that you do to help me make my visions for Arcade a reality for the readers! I look forward to all the exciting things God has in store for us, and for YOU!

The Zondervan/Zonderkidz Team—Sometimes I have to pinch myself to make sure this is really happening! YOU ALL ROCK! Keep up the great work. As I told you before, I am super-excited about this and future projects. I truly feel that though things are already AWESOME with this publishing relationship, the best is yet to come! You totally inspire me to want to keep sharing my life and gifts with the world, and especially with the kids!

Every kid who reads this book—If you read the first two books, or even if you haven't yet read done so, please know that I still see you. I still believe in you. You are still amazing. Let no one tell you otherwise. And if you're not already enjoying your own Arcade adventures, stick around. My buddy Arcade Livingston is sure to inspire you to get up and get after it. So enjoy this book, and be on the lookout for the next one. And as always, enjoy the ride!

Check out these other books in the Coin Slot Chronicles series:

And coming soon ...

Arcade and the Dazzling Truth Detector